JOHN RUSSELL FEARN'S
THE GOLDEN AMAZON

THE CRIMSON PERIL

JOHN RUSSELL FEARN'S
THE GOLDEN AMAZON

THE CRIMSON PERIL

JOHN GLASBY

The Golden Amazon, Book 23

WILDSIDE PRESS

INTRODUCTION

ONCE again, it gives me great pleasure to introduce another novel by John Glasby, the 29th title in this series of action-packed interstellar adventures, starring John Russell Fearn's most enduring character—Violet Ray Brant, alias *The Golden Amazon.*

This present work, *The Crimson Peril,* John's follow-up to his first Amazon novel, *Seetee Sun,* is special in two ways. Not only because of the sheer quality of its writing, in which Glasby has captured that elusive sense of wonder so redolent of Fearn's Amazon series, but because the story was actually inspired by another literary fragment written by Fearn himself. A fragment that no one, outside of myself, actually knew existed!

As regular followers of this series of novels will know, Fearn always *ended* his stories by writing the opening paragraphs of the *next* Amazon adventure, making one continuous cliff-hanging narrative. However, in 1959, for the very first time, the *Star Weekly* rejected Fearn's new Amazon novel, *Lords of Creation.* Whilst this was eventually published posthumously, the *ending* of this novel, when published, was in fact edited by myself, in order to lead smoothly into the next novel in the series.

I had to remove Fearn's original "pulsating crimson star" ending, and instead insert a few paragraphs of my own so that it that led directly into the next published novel.

At my request, Glasby had ended *Seetee Sun* on a clean finish. However, on remembering this unused ending/beginning, I typed it out and sent it to John Glasby, asking him to consider using it to start his next Amazon novel.

In the event, John was intrigued with the idea of using Fearn's opening, and more particularly was intrigued with the idea of a pulsating crimson star. It directly inspired the present novel, making it a truly authentic Amazon adventure, albeit written in Glasby's own style.

This happy collaboration was not really surprising. Fascinated by astronomy since childhood, Glasby joined the variable star section of the British Astronomical Society in 1958, being made its Director in 1965. He was elected a Fellow of the Royal astronomical Society in 1960 and went on to publish numerous textbooks and encyclopedias on astronomy, beginning with VARIABLE STARS in 1968. This astronomical and scientific background adds immensely to Glasby's own science fiction, and is manifest in the present novel.

As I noted in my introduction to SEETEE SUN, Glasby was the ideal choice of author to continue the Golden Amazon series, because, like Fearn, he had a treasure-chest of previously published material to draw upon for inspiration. In THE CRIMSON PERIL buffs of vintage British science fiction may detect definite resonances with Glasby's own very first novel, SATELLITE B.C. (1952) featuring the adventures of the crew of the interstellar exploration spaceship *Ultimate Thule*. But THE CRIMSON PERIL was essentially a brand-new work, and a worthy addition to the saga of the Golden Amazon.

—Philip Harbottle,
Wallsend, 2022.

CHAPTER I

THE Cosmic Crusaders, the *Ultra* under automatic control, sat in the broad well of the observation window gazing out onto the coldly unwinking stars of the Milky Way.

"And now what?" Viona asked. "A respite in space? A kind of cosmic holiday—?"

"Holidays never did anyone any real good," the ever-active Amazon answered briefly. "The end of one experience is but the beginning of another."

"Another—?" Abna asked, as she gazed into space. "Why, what have you in mind?"

"I'm interested in that," she responded, nodding her blonde head—and the others gazed with her in silent puzzlement and interest.

Perhaps half a light year away was a star, the most curious star ever. Dull red and pulsating like a living thing. It was behaving as no star should. For a long time the Crusaders looked at it, then Viona's eyes became mystified.

"What is it, anyway?" she asked. "Plainly it's a sun of some dull red color, since all stars are really suns—but what makes it carry on like that? Varying between first and tenth magnitude, beating like a living heart..."

"For such mysteries as this we travel the void." The Amazon smiled, then without another word she got up and crossed to the control board.

Under the manipulation of switches the vast nose of the *Ultra* slowly swung round in the deeps until it was pointed directly at the pulsating enigma in the depths.

Swiftly, unnoticeably, velocity increased.

"This is certainly something I've never seen before," said the Amazon musingly. Digging into her fantastic astronomical knowledge she went on, "Of course there are stars which do pulsate, their temperature varying with their diameter, but these cyclic changes take place in months or years—not minutes like this one and certainly by as much."

Turning from his examination of the star, Abna added, "There are also objects known as pulsars which emit very regular flashes of light and radio waves, but we now know these are really pairs of neutron stars, very close together and revolving extremely rapidly. These pulses are due to a rather complicated interaction between the surrounding material and their strong magnetic and gravitational fields. Plainly this is not one of them."

Thania, the teenager they had recruited during one of their recent adventures, rose from her chair and came to stand beside the Amazon. "Then what is it? A star like a beating heart in the middle of the galaxy! It just doesn't make sense."

"Oh, it makes sense," Abna glanced up at her. "It's simply that it is something we've never come across before and, at the moment, we don't have the answer to its odd behavior."

"So how do we go about finding out?" Viona ran a slim hand through her copper-gold hair. "Clearly if it's something inside that sun which is causing these peculiar oscillations, we can't take the *Ultra* into it to find out."

Pursing her lips, the Amazon replied, "That is certainly something I wouldn't like to attempt. Even though the surface temperature of that sun is only about 4000 degrees, much cooler than most stars, and the *Ultra* might be able to withstand that temperature for a very short time, the interior will be far hotter."

She turned her attention to the instrument board. "Let's see if the spectrum can tell us anything." Depressing a small switch, she waited for a moment until the band of glowing colors, crossed by a series of narrow black lines, came up on the display screen.

Both she and Abna ran expert eyes over the spectrum. Finally, Abna shook his head. "There seems to be nothing there to mark it out from millions of other cool red stars. The surface temperature drops slightly as it expands and then rises again as it contracts but that's quite normal."

"There is one thing about it which I do find strange." Mexone turned from examining the distant sun.

"What's that?" the Amazon asked.

"Well, my astronomical knowledge is not as extensive as yours but judging from its present condition, I would say that it has evolved far more quickly than other stars to reach the evolutionary stage it's at now."

Abna furrowed his brow in concentration. "Are you suggesting that someone has tinkered with the normal nuclear reactions going on inside that star and speeded them up in some way? I suppose anything is possible in the universe—but a race capable of doing that would be intellectually as far above us as we are above the amoeba."

Sighing in exasperation, the Amazon straightened. Reaching out, she flicked another switch that brought the large telescope into operation. On the huge visiscreen, the image of the distant sun expanded swiftly as she adjusted the controls. Even though they were prepared for it, the rapid expansion and contraction of the sun on the screen made them all momentarily dizzy. It was as if they were being flung forward and then backward at the same time.

Clamping a tight hold on her vision, the Amazon said quietly, "Do any of you notice anything strange about this image?"

"There are a small number of sunspots on the surface. I can make them out quite clearly," Mexone replied. "Surely there's nothing strange about that?"

"I think I know what you mean, mother," Viona said. "The image seems fuzzy around the edges."

"And no matter how I adjust the focus, it remains exactly the same. Therefore, this is no fault in the telescope. It has to be something else. It's as if the images are very slightly out of phase with each other."

"Meaning there's some kind of distortion in space around that sun?" Abna's broad brow was creased in puzzlement. "We've come across something like this around that seetee sun on the rim of the galaxy, but this spectrum is quite normal. There's nothing like that in this case."

"So it has to be something else," The Amazon retorted. "Something I intend to find out, but first I'd like to know whether there are any planets in this strange system. Remember, our first aim is to help any under-developed races in the galaxy. If there are none at all, then all this will accomplish is to merely satisfy our scientific curiosity."

"Do you think it's likely we'll find any planets around that sun?" Mexone queried. "From the very nature of that star I would say it's bound to be alone in space."

The Amazon shrugged her supple shoulders. "We won't know the answer to that question, Mexone, until we get much closer. My own guess would be that, even if there are any worlds revolving around that strange sun, we won't find any evidence of life."

She glanced at her husband as she spoke, saw Abna nod in agreement. "That sun must have a very low temperature even at its minimum diameter," Abna concurred. "You can tell that from its color—which means that any planet having life on it similar to ourselves would have to be very close to it."

"Would that be a problem?" Viona spoke up from the far side of the control board as she fed a copper bar into the *Ultra's* atomic power plant. "Some planets, like Uxxar which we found revolving around that seetee sun, do lie very close to their luminary."

"It would be quite a big problem in this case," the Amazon told her. "With that sun expanding and contracting like that, any planet sufficiently close to it to receive sufficient warmth would be alternately outside and inside it—merely warm one minute and searing hot the next. No, I think we can be reasonably sure this is a sterile system."

"There is one possibility," Abna said, "although it's one we've not come across before. Even though the temperature of that sun is pretty low, it must be emitting a tremendous amount of infrared radiation. We can't detect it with our eyes, of course, but like the microwaves they used on your planet, Vi, those rays do possess heat."

"So there is some doubt about the absence of any life here," nodded the Amazon. "Then this is certainly a system worthy of examination."

"Well, it's half a light year away, so we'll have to travel through hyperspace. I suggest we prepare ourselves for the transition."

Once this had been done, the Amazon set the relays into motion, automatically increasing the velocity without the intervention of any human hand. Pressed back into their sprung seats as the strain of the swiftly increasing acceleration took a hold on them, they allowed the flawless instruments on board the *Ultra* to take them towards the velocity of light.

Asleep in their seats, the five Crusaders remained oblivious to everything that was happening around them. More relays clicked into position and then, within a microsecond, the *Ultra* was enveloped by the tremendous energy flux which warped the vessel into the fourth dimension.

Here, time did not have the same meaning as in normal space-time. After approximately half a light year had been covered, the *Ultra* automatically slipped out of the fourth dimension and back into normal space. Still under the control of the intricate electronic brains, following the instructions which the Amazon had programmed into them, the forward retarding rockets came on, slowing the tremendous forward velocity which was still very close to that of light speed.

The Amazon recovered first and then Abna. By the time the Amazon had brought normal Earth gravity back into the vessel, the other three Crusaders were awake and alert.

Standing in front of the controls, Abna said casually, "Everything exactly right. There's that sun almost dead ahead."

On the huge screen the strange sun now dominated everything. Crowding in front of the forward viewer, the Crusaders scanned the scene, striving to pick out the smallest details. One minute the sun was just a small crimson disc; the next it had swelled like a balloon being blown up and then deflated. Around it was only the utter blackness of empty space.

"There doesn't seem to be anything within half a billion miles of the sun," Viona said, trying to keep the disappointment from her voice. "It looks as though you were right. This is just a strange, lonely sun moving through empty space."

It was Thania who spotted a planet first, letting out a whoop as she pointed excitedly.

Pressing herself forward against the controls, the Amazon directed her gaze to where the teenager was pointing. The tiny crescent was extremely faint and only just visible against the background of stars—and it was certainly not in the place she had expected to find any worlds in this enigmatic system.

Abna had seen it too. He shook his blond head in obvious puzzlement. Speaking quietly, he said, "If that is a planet, Thania, and it certainly looks like one, it's much further from that sun than I would have anticipated."

"It's certainly not one where I would expect to find life of any kind," the Amazon murmured, her full lips pursed. "The temperature on its surface must be close to absolute zero. Furthermore, there will be no atmosphere. Everything will be completely frozen onto the surface."

From the other side of the observation well, Viona suddenly called, "There's another planet. I can just make it out. At the moment it's very close to the sun. It seems to be moving behind it and it's only visible when that sun is at its smallest diameter."

The Crusaders watched intently as the strange sun swelled and contracted. As Viona had said, the tiny speck of light was just visible at regular intervals. It was clearly moving in an orbit that was now taking it out of sight behind the crimson disc.

The Amazon turned her head sharply from scrutinizing the outermost world. "So," she said finally, "Instead of finding no planets at all, there are at least two in this system. From the look of that other one, it seems to be closer to the sun than the one Thania noticed, perhaps about fifty million miles from the luminary. A possible candidate for some form of life, I suppose, but I think we'll leave that one for later."

Leaving the others, she moved back to the telescopic equipment, aligning the large telescope quickly on the tiny world that swung in its lonely outer orbit around the curious sun. The faintly glowing crescent came into sharp focus. At that tremendous distance it received very little light from the sun.

A moment later, she uttered a sharp exclamation. The others turned away from the large observation screen. "What is it, Vi?" Abna asked.

"Something I would never have expected. I would have been certain that it's a foregone conclusion that nothing could live on that frozen world. But unless there's a fault in the telescopic system, which I doubt, there's a fleet of spacecraft leaving that planet and heading sunward."

She moved aside as Abna came over to her. Swiftly, he peered at the screen; then flicked a switch that increased the magnification to the highest possible. A second switch immediately transferred the enlarged image onto the massive visiscreen. Now they were all able to see what the Amazon had picked out.

Beside the planetary disc, the formation of tiny points of light was just visible. Even so, there was no doubt in any of their minds that these pinpricks of light represented the exhausts from spacecraft. Staring at them with a bemused expression on her face, Viona muttered, "Then in spite of what we originally thought, that world must be inhabited."

"But surely that is impossible," Mexone said incredulously. "You're suggesting we've come across a race that can live at a temperature of almost absolute zero. This must certainly be a first for the Crusaders. In fact I'd say it's a first in the whole field of science. You were right, Amazon. That planet is something which needs looking into, if only to satisfy our natural scientific curiosity as to how such a race can possibly survive."

On the large screen, the tight knot of dots seemed to move at a snail's pace. But they all knew this was merely an illusion caused by the tremendous distance. In reality, those spaceships were moving away from the planet with a tremendous velocity.

Over the minutes, they studied the trajectory of the alien ships and it soon became clear that the *Ultra* had not been spotted for the vessels held an undeviating course in the direction of the pulsating sun.

Reaching a decision, the Amazon said, "Keep a close watch on those vessels, Viona. We'll give them time to leave that area of space and then we'll approach that planet from this direction. I'd like to know a little more of what we've got here before risking an encounter with them."

Over the ensuing minutes it became apparent that the alien spacecraft were still maintaining their straight, undeviating course. Clearly, whoever was on board them was totally unaware of their presence. For the time being the *Ultra* had remained undetected.

Manipulating the controls, Abna then diverted the thrust of the engines to the forward rockets. Gradually, the *Ultra* decelerated until they were almost stationary in space.

Finally, the Amazon was satisfied that the distant spaceships were sufficiently far from the planet for them to proceed. "We'll approach this world from the spaceward side," she decided crisply. "If those space travelers are inhabitants of this planet there may be others down there and this way we stand less chance of being seen."

Nodding in silent agreement, Abna increased their velocity slightly, turning the *Ultra* through a wide arc. By the time the planetary crescent had swelled to almost fill the visiscreen they were traveling at a modest 20,000 miles an hour. Beside him, the Amazon flicked a switch, putting the *Ultra* into a stable decelerating orbit around the planet.

Glancing up, Abna studied the series of figures that appeared on the subsidiary screen. These provided them with accurate details of the planetary characteristics. Reeling them off, he said, "Diameter thirty-one thousand miles, a little larger than Earth. Surface temperature just a degree above absolute zero. There is no detectable atmosphere, which isn't surprising since all of it will be frozen onto the surface. There might just be a little liquid helium but that's all."

"Obviously this is one of the most inhospitable worlds we've ever visited," Viona put in. There was a trace of disappointment in her voice. "I doubt if it will be possible for us to land there and go outside the *Ultra* to look around. We would all be frozen stiff within seconds at that temperature."

"Nevertheless, those spaceships we spotted came from here," Abna reminded her.

Seating herself again, the Amazon said firmly, "Not necessarily. And if this race are simply space travelers exploring this system, they may have decided that nothing can possibly live there and it's of no interest to them. There would be no need for them to land here. They could see for themselves from space what the surface conditions are like. Now they could be moving sunward towards that second planet."

"So if they do live in this planetary system, it's almost certain they came from there," Mexone suggested.

Smiling, the Amazon said, "Possible, Mexone. When you're dealing with the galaxy, nothing is certain—or even almost certain."

"Then don't you think we would be simply wasting time examining this one?" Thania put the blunt question directly to the Amazon. "Surely our time would be much better spent trying to discover why this sun is behaving as it does."

The Amazon gave a decisive shake of her blonde head. "If we can find a suitable place, I'm all for landing and investigating this planet at first hand. As for going outside, Viona, that won't pose too big a problem. We have means of heating our insulated spacesuits to a bearable temperature despite the external conditions down there."

While Mexone took out the specially insulated suits from the cupboards, Abna and Thania studied the surface of the planet as the *Ultra* passed over it. The frozen atmosphere formed a highly reflective surface in the starlight. Far larger than Pluto, it nevertheless bore a striking resemblance to the outermost planet of the Solar System. Virtually the whole of the surface was flat with few distinct features, broken only by deep cracks of problematical depth. There were, however, a small number of large craters, their circular rims just visible above the layer of frozen gases. There were also two long ranges of high mountains, all completely covered with a white coating of atmospheric ice.

On the far side, however, they came upon curious markings, which, even at first sight, appeared to be artificial. There were peculiar crisscrossing rifts, some extending deep into the ground, as if part of the surface had been gouged out by a huge knife. Scanning them, Abna remarked, "What do you make of those, Vi? To me it almost looks as though large-scale mining operations have been taking place down there."

Glancing around his broad shoulder, the Amazon allowed her violet-eyed gaze to study the odd features minutely. "It certainly looks that way to me," she agreed finally. "But why would anyone want to remove frozen atmospheric gases and rock and where have they been taken? Some of those markings seem to have been made quite recently, certainly long after the atmosphere froze. If you look down there, the underlying rock is still clearly visible. This is definitely something we must look into."

At the table, Mexone called, "I've computed the orbit of this world, Amazon. It seems to be highly elliptical just like Pluto in your solar system, and it has a year equivalent to approximately three hundred of your Earth years."

The Amazon gave a brief nod. "That means that at three hundred yearly intervals it will be sufficiently close to this sun for at least some of this frozen surface to melt and then vaporize, possibly providing it with an atmosphere of sorts. At the moment, it seems to be at its furthest point from the luminary."

"So we can't expect anything like summer on this world for more than a century," Thania said with a trace of disappointment in her voice.

"Afraid not," smiled the Amazon. "Now let's get down there and see what we can find. I'm particularly interested in what those other spacefarers were doing here."

Abna's voice held a note of caution as he said, "Before we even think of landing on that surface, there is one thing I have to check."

Shrugging into her suit, the Amazon paused. "What's that? Something we've overlooked?"

In reply, Abna pointed towards the smooth surface over which they were traveling. "It's imperative we determine the depth of that frozen layer. Once we land the heat from the *Ultra's* exhaust will melt that instantly. It could be highly dangerous if we were to sink into it to any appreciable depth. At the moment we have no idea how thick that covering of frozen atmosphere is. I wouldn't like to land the *Ultra* there and find ourselves sinking through a hundred feet of it."

"Good thinking, Abna," Mexone said. "I'll check it with the sonar. That should give us the answer in a few minutes."

The *Ultra* was now cruising slowly over the smooth region at a height of fifty thousand feet. Even though the sonar beam transmitted from the *Ultra* was completely invisible, it nevertheless enabled them to build up a complete picture of the nature of the ground beneath the layer of frozen atmosphere.

At the end of fifteen minutes, they had mapped the topography of the solid ground under the layer of hydrogen, oxygen and methane ice. The glacial covering varied between two and five feet in thickness and beneath it was solid rock.

"It's much better than I had feared," Abna confirmed. "If we land at an angle, we should clear away most of that ice giving us a solid surface to stand on."

"Then go ahead," the Amazon said with a note of impatience in her tone. She could understand her husband's natural caution, but the enigma of this curious world and its highly peculiar sun now intrigued her to the point where she was anxious to discover more about both.

"Any particular place you'd like me to put the *Ultra* down?" Abna inquired without taking his attention from the controls.

The Amazon made up her mind immediately. "As close as you can to those peculiar markings in the surface. I'm anxious to know if they have been artificially made."

Handling the controls with his usual dexterity, Abna reduced the *Ultra's* velocity still further and a few moments later there was a slight bump, and they were sliding across the surface. A few moments later, the *Ultra* came to a smooth stop. Behind them lay a wide, two-mile-long swathe where the friction had melted the frozen atmosphere that had then almost immediately vaporized in a silent explosion. A white cloud of tiny particles hung momentarily above the ground before falling back again.

Ten minutes later they had all donned their protective insulated suits, adjusting the internal temperature to that on board the *Ultra*. Stepping into the airlock, they waited for a moment until the outer door opened automatically. The short ladder unfolded itself until it rested on the exposed pale grey rock.

With the gravity only slightly higher than that of Earth, they experienced no difficulty in climbing down and moving around. Over their heads the sky was jet black with thousands of stars glittering in alien constellations. Just above the distant horizon, the sun was little more than a bright star still exhibiting its peculiar pulsations, expanding and contracting in a regular manner that was almost hypnotic.

In the distance, perhaps twenty miles away, high sharply peaked mountains formed a formidable barrier in that direction. Everywhere else there was nothing but the perfectly smooth surface—except for the deep indentations that lay not more than a quarter of a mile away.

Over the tiny radio in her helmet, one of the Amazon's technological marvels which operated even in a total vacuum, transforming speech into light and then back again in the receiver, Viona said, "Evidently those odd changes in the sun don't have any noticeable effect on the temperature here."

"At this distance they would be so small we probably wouldn't be able to measure them," the Amazon replied.

After a slight pause, Thania said, "It's hard to visualize an entire planet that is completely dead."

"You have to remember that once the temperature gets down very close to absolute zero there's hardly any movement of the molecules." Abna explained. "You reach a state of complete absence of motion. There are no interactions between the atoms. Everything is virtually static. Don't you agree, Vi?"

There was no reply. The Amazon was already pushing her way through the crust of hard-packed ice. Slowly, the others followed. In places it came almost up to their waists. Fortunately, the material of their suits was sufficiently strong and flexible not to be pierced or damaged by the occasional sharp edges. At times, however, they had to smash through the ice with their clenched fists where the frozen covering seemed almost as hard as iron.

Even with their superhuman strength, the journey to their objective proved tiring. At last, however, they stood on the edge of the nearest rift, looking down into the completely dark depths. Taking her atomic-powered torch from her belt, the Amazon shone the intense beam of light down into the abyss that yawned at her feet.

Slowly, she played the beam around the steep rocky walls taking careful note of the straight ridges. Finally straightening and uttering an exclamation of satisfaction, she said. "This is just what I suspected. All this rock has been mechanically removed. But for what purpose, I can't imagine."

"Perhaps it contains some chemical element those spaceships we saw need as fuel for their engines," Viona suggested, "just as we use copper in the *Ultra*."

"That could be the answer, I suppose," murmured the Amazon, "especially if there are any radioactive elements in this material."

"Is that likely?" Thania asked.

"We'll soon find out." Replacing the torch in her belt, the Amazon took out the Geiger counter unit and pointed it directly into the looming hole. When she pressed the stud, the instrument uttered a few desultory clicks and the needle, visible in the light of the torch in Abna's hand, scarcely quivered.

"There's very little radioactivity," she said finally. "It's just about the same as you would find if you examined normal rocks from Earth."

"Nonetheless, mother," Viona commented. "With the necessary extraction equipment, it would be quite simple to purify whatever uranium or other radioactive element is present."

The Amazon thought that over before replying, "So at the moment all we know is that a race from some other planet comes here at intervals to carry out mining operations." There was a trace of disappointment in her voice. "There's nothing strange or irregular about that. The scientists on Earth have been doing exactly the same for decades, mining the planets and their moons for valuable metals. I was somehow hoping that—"

Abna stared at her through the transparent faceplate of his helmet. "I know exactly what you were hoping for, Vi," he interrupted. "You were hoping that here we might meet up with some belligerent race intent on planetary conquest. Instead, we've merely stumbled upon an ordinary mining operation being carried out on an uninhabited world."

The Amazon did not reply. She had moved a short distance away and was minutely examining the rock at the edge of the steep drop. There was a puzzled frown on her beautiful features. When she looked up it was as if she had not heard Abna's statement.

"This rock," she said decisively. "Unless I'm mistaken it's an igneous rock. That means there must have been volcanic activity here at some time in the past."

"So what's important about that?" Thania inquired. "All of that may have happened millions of years ago. We saw no sign of any volcanoes when we approached this planet."

The Amazon straightened. "That's true—because as you say it probably happened in the distant past. But the fact that it did happen means that this world may still have a molten core. It certainly explains the fact that the gravity is Earthlike."

"But Pluto, which is the only planet like this that I've ever visited," Viona put in, "doesn't have a molten core."

"Of course not," the Amazon explained. "Pluto is a far smaller world. Some have even described it as nothing more than a gigantic snowball. Others think it may once have been a satellite of Neptune which somehow broke away and went flying off into its own highly eccentric orbit around Sol."

"Then what is so important about this world having a molten core?" Mexone asked, a puzzled frown on his face.

"Just think about it for a moment." There was an expression of subdued excitement in the Amazon's violet eyes now. "A molten core means that it may be a lot warmer down there under all of this ice and rock. It could possibly be warm enough to support life."

Some of her excitement transferred itself to the other Crusaders. After a long, reflective pause, Abna said, "You may be right, Vi. I know it sounds fantastic—but I must admit it is possible."

"Then I think we should start looking right away," Thania exclaimed.

"Don't let your youthful enthusiasm run away with you, Thania," the Amazon admonished gently. "So far this is only a theory. I think we should return to the ship, have a meal, and discuss it objectively."

Turning, they walked back to where the massive shape of the *Ultra* rested on the ice. They were only halfway there when Mexone gave a sudden shout which brought them all to a standstill.

"What is it?" the Amazon asked, coming up to him and scanning the terrain around them. She could see nothing out of the ordinary to account for his obvious excitement.

He was pointing to their left. "What can that be?"

Following the direction of his gloved hand, they noticed something projecting from the smooth plain perhaps thirty yards away. Thrusting his way towards it, Abna bent and examined the object closely. It was a stout rod made of some kind of metal with a small rectangular box on the top.

Grasping it carefully, he gave it an experimental pull but in spite of his tremendous strength it resisted all of his efforts to free it. "Whatever it is, it seems to be firmly embedded in the rock under this ice."

Going down beside him, the Amazon ran her fingers over it. Carefully, she used her gloved hands to scrape away much of the ice around it, finally exposing the bare rock. Behind the transparent mask of her helmet, her face was twisted into a look of concentration. Finally, she said, "I would say that this goes all the way through the rock, possibly for miles. My guess is that it's some kind of remote temperature recorder. The question is—who put it here—and why?

If it is still functioning, it must be transmitting data to someone—somewhere."

"Someone deep underground?" Viona suggested.

"Either that, or to whoever was on board those spaceships we saw earlier. We can't rule out the possibility that they put it here for some scientific purpose." She rose smoothly to her feet. "This planetary system gets more curious all the time. Why would anyone want to monitor the temperature out here in the middle of this frozen waste? It won't vary by more than a hundredth of a degree for centuries."

"But it will change when this planet approaches that sun in its strange orbit," Thania put in. "Then the external temperature might be important to someone."

"Evidently you don't have much to learn," the Amazon commended. "But why should anyone—?"

A sudden warning shout from Viona brought them all whirling round and stopped the Amazon in mid-sentence. "I thought 1 saw something moving!" she cried.

"I don't see anything." Mexone stared around him in all directions.

There was nothing to be seen. The smooth surface gleamed faintly in the starlight.

Then, perhaps twenty feet away, the solid ice began shifting in the most peculiar manner. It twisted and spun as if a miniature tornado had struck it. But in a completely airless world that was, of course, impossible.

Nevertheless, the ice was rising swiftly and forming into a semi-humanoid shape. It possessed a broad torso and what looked like a multitude of whip-like tentacles protruding from its middle. Exuding a bitter, penetrating cold it moved slowly and silently in their direction.

"What can it be?" Thania asked in an awe-struck tone.

"It's something I would never have believed possible." Abna, too, seemed unable to believe his senses. "At this temperature, all molecular vibrations and interactions should have virtually stopped. Yet there seems to be some kind of intelligence here making that thing function."

"My God," This time it was Mexone who yelled. "There are more of them between us and the *Ultra*!"

Turning their heads wildly, the Crusaders saw that what he said was true. About a dozen of the creatures had suddenly appeared, rising from the surface and forming a menacing line across the ice. Swiftly, the Amazon drew her gun and aimed it at the nearest creature. The narrow beam of pure energy struck the thing in the middle.

But instead of incapacitating it in any way, the beam merely passed right through it and a moment later the dark hole closed and became whole again. Sucking in a deep breath, Abna called, "It's obvious we can't kill these creatures with our blasters. They simply absorb the energy of the beam."

"Then what else is there we can use?" Now there was a faint trace of hysteria in Thania's voice. "If these guns won't stop them, nothing will."

By now the creatures were less than ten yards away. Those at each end of the line moved more quickly than the others and it was clear they intended to encircle them. The mere fact of this obvious maneuver was sufficient to tell the Crusaders that these creatures were not entirely mindless.

For a moment, the Amazon stared down at the useless weapon in her gloved hand. Then she snapped harshly, "If our weapons have no effect, there's only one thing that may—sheer, brute force."

Before she finished speaking, she was running forward as quickly as possible over the slippery, treacherous ground. Bracing herself, she slammed into one of the creatures, her shoulder crashing into it with all her strength behind the blow. For an instant, the thing remained upright.

The next moment it shattered into a hundred flying fragments that fell rapidly to the ground. Momentarily, the Amazon glimpsed something like a tiny red globe that dropped onto the ice at her feet as she fought to keep her balance. Whatever it was, it vanished within seconds as if it had burrowed deep into the ice.

Seeing the success of her action, the others did likewise. Striding forward, swinging his right arm in a short arc, Abna delivered a literally shattering blow at the creature confronting him. A second sideways swipe of his fist had the same effect on another of the monsters as it tried to lunge at him. Ignoring those behind him, he grabbed the Amazon's arm and hustled her towards the *Ultra.* Two more splintered into fragments as Viona grabbed them around the middle and swung them together with a powerful pull of her arms.

With the way temporarily open, they raced for the *Ultra*. Reaching the bottom of the ladder, the Amazon turned as Mexone and Viona came thrusting forward through the knee-deep ice. It was only then that they noticed Thania was not with them. She had smashed one of the lumbering monsters into flying shards of ice with her fists but had failed to notice the two others that had moved up swiftly behind her.

Now she was lying face down on the ice and one of them had wrapped its tentacles tightly around her middle. Without thinking, the Amazon and Abna ran forward. Raising both her gloved hands, the Amazon brought them down with pile-driver force on the two creatures bending over Thania.

Like the others, they disintegrated instantly under the blows. As she straightened, Abna bent and turned Thania over. Beneath his gloved fingers her body was completely rigid, as solid as an iron bar. Through the transparent helmet, he could just see that her face was pure white. Her eyes were wide open, but it was evident she could not see him.

"What is it, Abna?" the Amazon asked anxiously, keeping an eye on the few remaining creatures that had moved some distance away, somehow aware that these strangers had the means of destroying them.

"We have to get her inside the *Ultra*—and quickly," Abna replied as he bent and picked Thania from the ice. "My guess is that she's frozen solid. Somehow those tentacles have the power to drain all of the heat away, even through these protective suits."

"Is she dead?"

Abna paused and then said slowly and somberly, "I don't know, Vi. I'd say her body temperature is now close to absolute zero and she's certainly in a near-death condition."

"But you can save her? You've done it before."

While they had been speaking, Abna had carried the stiff body of the teenager to the ladder leading into the *Ultra's* main airlock, still keeping a wary eye on the remaining creatures.

Climbing quickly, he carried Thania inside. Behind him, the Amazon raised the ladder and hauled the airlock shut, closing it securely.

In the observation well, Abna laid Thania's body on the table. "Keep her suit on. It's essential that we raise her body temperature very slowly otherwise we may cause fatal internal damage," he said. "Once we've done that, I'll see what I can do for her. I'm not fully recovered from that trudging through the ice, and this will take a lot of mental concentration."

"I'm sure you'll do everything you possibly can," Viona said softly, slipping out of her own suit. Going to the table, she helped the Amazon check the temperature inside Thania's suit, taking great care how they moved the frozen body.

Looking down at the stiff, white face and staring, sightless eyes, the Amazon knew it would test all of her husband's metaphysical skill to save the teenager. It was the one faculty she had never learned and sometimes she inwardly resented the fact that in this particular field, he undoubtedly surpassed her.

Very slowly, under the Amazon's expert eye, Thania's body attained the temperature inside the *Ultra*. Only then did they gently remove the suit to allow Abna to examine her. His handsome features creased in taut concentration as he employed all of his metaphysical power to check and repair any damage the teenager had suffered; ruptured arteries and organs where even the blood had crystallized, internal bleeding and a host of other internal injuries.

It was slow and painstaking work. A quarter of an hour passed and still there seemed no response. Finally, however, he drew himself up to his full height. "She'll be fine now," he said, smiling a little despite the effort it had cost him.

On the table, Thania opened her eyes, staring around her as if unable to comprehend where she was. Then she pushed herself up onto her arms. "What happened? I remember smashing one of those creatures out there. Then something caught me round the waist and... and I don't remember anything else."

"That thing—whatever it was—drained every bit of heat out of you," the Amazon explained. "How they can do that and yet maintain themselves at a low enough temperature to prevent their bodies from melting, I don't know but your body was at almost absolute zero when we brought you in here."

"Then how—?"

"Don't worry your head about it now," Abna said gently. "You're fully recovered and now I think we should all have a meal and discuss everything we've found here."

CHAPTER II

THE question of whether it was possible that there might be a race living in the interior of this world and if so how to contact them, was uppermost in their minds while they ate, going over the theory that the Amazon had suggested. At first, it had seemed nothing more than an extremely remote possibility but with the discovery of that temperature detecting device, it was now looking more and more plausible.

It was Abna who spoke first. "I think we should begin by making the assumption that you're right, Vi. If you're wrong, any further discussion would be futile. So, if this planet is inhabited by more advanced beings than those creatures we met out there, the only place anyone can exist is deep underground where they can benefit from the warmth of a molten core. How they have succeeded in doing that is beyond me at the moment."

"It would certainly be a tremendous feat of engineering to perform something like that on a planetary scale," Mexone remarked.

"That isn't the kind of life which would appeal to me," Thania said from across the table. "I can't imagine how depressing it must be, never being in the open air, never seeing anything outside, possibly living in almost perpetual darkness."

The Amazon smiled. "It may not be very different from living in the confined space of the *Ultra*."

"Yes, but at least we can see the stars and visit new worlds."

"Of course we can," the Amazon acknowledged gently. "But coming back to our main theme, we've met many different races during our travels through the galaxy but most of these have been surface-dwellers."

Mexone leaned forward over the table. "I think that such people must have a high degree of intelligence and technological achievement even to exist under these extreme circumstances, completely sealed off from the outside world."

"And that temperature recorder we discovered," the Amazon said. "If they are completely sealed off, they may want to record any changes in the outside temperature."

"But why?" Mexone was still mystified.

"My guess is that at those times when this planet approaches sufficiently close to that sun yonder, it may be possible that all of this frozen stuff will melt sufficiently to provide an atmosphere so they can live on the surface, if only for a short time."

"So then they may know something about this stellar system," Abna said. "Their sojourn on the surface would not last for very long, possibly for only a few years—but certainly sufficient for them to make some observations."

"Then if we can find them and make contact, they may be able to tell us about this other race," Viona put in. "They may even have an explanation for the peculiar behavior of that sun."

"So all we have to do is find some way into this world and that won't be easy." Thania pushed her empty plate away. She had now fully recovered from her ordeal.

"I agree," Abna replied. "Even if there is an entrance to some inner world, it will certainly be extremely well concealed, not only as a protection against that other race but also from those creatures on the surface. It could take us ages to search every bit of this world and even then—" He broke off abruptly.

Who are you? The words sounded clearly in all of their minds, as clearly as if they had been spoken aloud.

As they stared at each other in complete surprise, the Amazon said softly, "It's some form of telepathic communication and in our own language."

Swiftly overcoming his initial confusion, Abna used his own considerable telepathic ability. "We are known as the Cosmic Crusaders, travelers from a star so distant you could not pick it out from the millions of others in the galaxy." He spoke the words for the benefit of the others.

What is your purpose here, Cosmic Crusaders? came the reply in their minds.

This time, it was the Amazon who consciously projected her thoughts. As Abna had done, she spoke aloud for the benefit of the others. Although not as inherently telepathic like Abna, she had the feeling that whoever was contacting them in this way could read the thought behind her spoken words quite clearly. "We roam the galaxy, seeking out oppressed or backward races in order that we may use our advanced science to help them fight against cruel and warlike people."

There was a long silence as if whoever was in contact with them had paused to consider this reply. Then the mental voice came again.

From the abrupt change in temperature on the surface we detected your presence on Xendor the moment your spaceship landed. At first, we thought you were that other race which seeks to destroy us.

"Then how is it you can understand us like this?" Abna put his words into thoughts.

We have absorbed your language from your minds in order that we may satisfy ourselves as to who you are and why you are here.

"Then you will know that we mean you no harm." The Amazon projected the words in her mind.

For a moment there was silence. Then: *We have reached a decision. Please remain where you are. None of you will be harmed.*

"What do they mean—remain where we are?" Viona asked, speaking aloud.

The Amazon gave a grim smile. "I think we are about to find out."

There was a sudden sinking sensation. Through the large screen, they saw the surface outside begin to rise. Then there was solid rock all around them, shutting off all sight of the stars. Slowly, the *Ultra* sank through the rock, dropping into the depths.

"We're going down into the planet!" Thania uttered the words in sudden alarm. "Where are they taking us?"

"It would seem they are taking us into their world," Abna said tightly. "Now all we can do is sit here and see what happens. The *Ultra* can travel through space but there is no way it can blast off through solid rock."

The spaceship descended through stratum after stratum with a steady velocity.

Then, abruptly, there was light all around them. It was a warm, yellow glow that bathed the interior of the observation well like normal sunlight. Getting swiftly to her feet, Thania ran to the windows, the other Crusaders following.

Outside was a vast open space, so huge that it was impossible to see the furthermost boundaries. Down below, as if hanging in the void, floated what could only be described as a planet.

Her sapphire-blue eyes wide with amazement, Viona called, "Why it's like an entire world inside a world."

"From what I can see," Mexone added, "that is exactly what it is. A new world built inside the outer shell of this planet. Look—it even has its own sun." He pointed to where a brilliant yellow globe hung high against the rocky roof, apparently suspended in midair. "And there are clouds down there and what look like continents and seas."

"Incredible." The Amazon spoke softly as if to herself. Speaking more loudly, she said, "You were absolutely right, Mexone, when you suggested this race has attained a high level of science and technology. But we must be careful not to make premature judgments about them. These people may not be all they seem."

Abna tore his gaze from the astonishing scene outside and returned to the controls. Pulling the switch at the front of the curving control board, he waited briefly for the mighty engines to operate. When there was no response, he tried again. Finally, with a shrug of his broad shoulders, he said in a puzzled tone. "The engines are not responding. Some force has us in its grip and is preventing us from using them."

"Whatever it is, it is clearly drawing us down to that world below," Thania exclaimed. "I can see what look like cities and towns. There is also a wide clear space. We seem to be being drawn towards that."

There was no time to pursue any further discussion. As lightly as a feather, the tremendous bulk of the *Ultra* slowly descended until, with scarcely a bump, they were resting on the large open area that Thania had spotted. Once they were safely down, Abna turned to examine the instruments.

With an expression of faint surprise, he said, "There is an atmosphere outside. From the analysis of its constituents, I would say it very closely approximates that of your home world, Vi. We should be able to go outside without wearing suits."

"And what is the temperature like out there?" Viona inquired.

"That's Earth-normal also."

Ever impatient to be doing something positive, the Amazon said harshly, "Then I suggest we go out and make contact with these people. But all of you take your weapons. This may not be quite what it looks. On Earth there is an old saying: Beware Greeks bearing gifts."

All but Abna looked puzzled by this remark, but they said nothing as they fastened their belts. Locking the controls, Abna followed the others towards the middle of the *Ultra*. Pressing the button of the airlock they waited until the pressures had equalized and the outer door had swung open. One after the other, they made their way down the short ladder, finally standing in a small group, their hands close to their weapons.

In the distance, tall, graceful buildings lined wide streets and nearer at hand, a slender stone bridge spanned a swiftly flowing river. Trees and bushes grew in abundance. Fountains threw sparkling cascades of water high into the air. Multi-colored birds flew among the flower-laden branches. People were everywhere.

Staring around in sheer wonder, Viona murmured, "This is how I imagine paradise must look—or the Garden of Eden."

Nodding gravely, the Amazon replied, "First impressions can often be wrong, Viona. Remember that the Garden of Eden was a virtual paradise, but it contained the Serpent."

"There's someone coming," Thania pointed. "From here, they look very like ourselves."

The members of the small group that approached were certainly humanoid in general appearance. All of them were old with lined features but they held themselves stiffly erect. One of them carried a long staff in his right hand, on the top of which glowed a large multi-faceted crystal. A myriad colored flashes speared in all directions as the light of the artificial sun caught it.

Advancing towards the five Crusaders, the man raised the staff and pointed it directly at them. Instantly, Abna's hand dived for the protonic blaster at his waist. He had half drawn it when the Amazon hissed sharply. "There is no need for weapons, Abna. I feel sure these people intend us no harm."

"You are quite correct in that supposition," the man said speaking in perfect English.

"You are evidently not that other race which comes here to steal our frozen atmosphere and rocks. All of this we have learned from your minds, and that is a universal way of obtaining the truth."

"And that is how you can speak our language." Even Abna, whose mental capabilities enabled him to extract an alien language within minutes from other races, looked astonished.

The ever-practical Amazon, however, went straight to the point. The fact that they could converse with these people in English was a definite bonus, but she had more important matters on her mind.

"You speak of this other race," she said briskly. "Why would they want to steal rocks and the frozen atmosphere? And perhaps more importantly, who are they and where do they come from? On the way here from space, we noticed a fleet of spacecraft leaving this planet and heading in the direction of the sun."

She had already dismissed from her mind the possibility that this other race was those ice creatures they had encountered.

One of the other men stepped forward, his lined features cast in a grave expression. "Those would be their spacecraft you saw but as to who they are and where they come from, we have no knowledge." He paused; then waved a hand towards the buildings in the near distance. "But we cannot talk out here. Come with us and we will tell you all we know."

"Your spacecraft will be quite safe," the leader assured them. What passed for a smile twisted his thin lips. "We have never mastered the art of building spacecraft and there is no one on Xendor who would know how to operate one. You were, however, under our control while you landed here which is why your engines did not operate."

As they walked towards the nearest building, the man with the staff said, "My name is Idron. I am the leader of what you would call the Council of Xendor. I speak for all the people. My companions, Credor, Meldon and Tremar are members of the Council. You could say that we are the law on this world."

"Do you know absolutely nothing of other suns and worlds out there in the galaxy?" Viona asked.

"We know of them," Meldon replied as he led the way up a flight of steps into a large open area surrounded by tall, ornate pillars. "There are certain times when our world approaches very close to the sun. Then our atmosphere returns and it is sufficiently warm for us to venture onto the surface. Unfortunately, that is the time of greatest danger for us."

As always, the Amazon's sharp mind had jumped to the obvious conclusion. "That is when you can be attacked by this other race."

"Exactly. We are not a warlike people; we desire no other world belonging to another race and so we possess no weapons with which to defend ourselves. We hoped to go unnoticed by any others. But now it seems that enemies have come and only when we are here, inside this thick shell which surrounds us are we relatively safe from them."

There was a pause as they seated themselves around a large table. Although none of the men spoke, a much younger woman, dressed in a flowing white robe, appeared with food and drink which she set down in front of them.

"But recently," continued Tremar, "they have increased the intensity of their attacks. Now they come more often, bombarding the upper surface with missiles in an attempt to break through and destroy us."

"I wonder," Abna mused, "if sheer wanton destruction is their real intention? That doesn't seem logical for a highly scientific race."

"I agree," the Amazon commented. "It's much more likely that their real object is to learn the scientific secrets of your inner world. How you maintain your artificial sun, and your control of atomic processes, for instance. They may have a desperate need of appropriating your technology for their own ends."

Idron looked troubled. "If that is the case, we are facing a terrible danger. They will keep trying until they succeed."

"Then this is something we must put a stop to," the Amazon declared heatedly, "and as soon as possible."

"But what can you do?" Idron asked. "You are but five with only one spacecraft. They are many."

"We've succeeded against far greater odds than that," Abna answered. "But first we have to know everything you call tell us about them—for example, where their home world might be."

Idron shook his head slowly. "That is one thing we cannot tell you. No one knows where they come from or where they go. They appear without warning and vanish just as quickly. Our attempts to read their minds have been unsuccessful. They keep their thoughts shielded."

"Then the only possibility is that they come from that second planet or some other stellar system," the Amazon remarked, "unless there are any additional planets in your system which we've somehow missed in our preliminary survey." She glanced at Abna. "That is something we'll have to check."

For a moment there was silence. Then Viona asked, "How did you transport us here through all of that solid rock? It seems too much of a coincidence that we were placed just on top of some kind of elevator."

Idron gave a solemn smile. "There is really no mystery about that. After all, what are all atoms made of? An extremely small positively charged nucleus and a number of even smaller electrons orbiting it. Therefore, ninety-nine percent of the atomic volume is empty space."

A puzzled frown creased Thania's forehead. "Then if that's true, why don't we simply fall through everything?"

"It's because these particles which go to make up everything are not like tiny, ultramicroscopic balls, they're smeared out like waves," explained the Amazon. "They're also in continuous, extremely rapid, motion so there's no time for us to fall through as you put it."

"Yet you seem to have achieved it," Abna said, looking directly at Idron.

"Yes. Long ago we discovered a means of halting the electrons in their orbits around the nucleus. That is, of course, a highly unstable condition. Being oppositely charged the electrons would simply fall into the nucleus and the atoms would then collapse completely. But this condition lasts only for the minutest fraction of a second. Nevertheless, we can perform it progressively from atom to atom and molecule to molecule so that any object will pass through any other as we will it."

"We do something similar on board our spaceship whenever we wish to become invisible to an enemy," the Amazon acknowledged. "In this case we align all of the electrons horizontally within the atoms and molecules so that light passes through and there is no reflection from the surface."

Gazing around at the splendid city outside, Abna noticed that the shadows of the buildings and people on the streets were slowly shortening. In the artificial sky, the 'sun' had altered its position. A cloud momentarily passed over it, sending a shadow hastening over the streets and buildings.

To the Amazon, he remarked, "Seeing all of this reminds me of your home world, Vi. Indeed, if it weren't for the peculiar circumstances in which we've found ourselves, I could believe it is Earth."

For a moment, a feeling of nostalgia passed through the Amazon, but she dismissed it at once. Earth was so far distant that she had almost forgotten it. For her, such homesick thoughts were a weakness that she repudiated at once.

She realized that Credor was speaking and forced herself to concentrate on his words. "Even though we are entombed within this shell of rock, we strove to make everything as it was, countless generations ago, when Xendor was much closer to the sun. There was an atmosphere then and the sun was not as it is now."

Viona's sapphire blue eyes widened, expressing surprise. "Then your sun has not always pulsated like a beating heart?"

Credor shook his head. "No, not at all. But then, so long ago that no one now alive on Xendor can remember it, our sun was just a normal star like countless others. Why—or how—it changed, we do not know. It was about that time that something happened to send our world far out into the depths until, instead of revolving in a circular orbit, it now travels in this strange elliptical one."

"All stars evolve, just like people, but over millions of years," Mexone put in. "Perhaps that is all that happened."

"Somehow, I don't think that is the answer," the Amazon said musingly. "From what these people are telling us, it happened quite suddenly."

"Then what is the answer?" Thania asked.

"I wish I knew. Of one thing I am certain. We won't find it here."

Finishing the meal, Abna asked, "Do you know anything of those creatures on the surface? They attacked us while we were outside our spaceship."

After a pause, Idron said, "We know a little of them although we have never encountered them ourselves. During that brief period when we can go out onto the surface, we believe they hibernate somewhere within the rocks. The warmth then would certainly kill them."

"We know them as the Drexei," Tremar put in. "Whether they possess any kind of intelligence, or act purely by instinct, we do not know. We have no knowledge of how they first appeared on this world. All we do know is that they are extremely dangerous. You would do well to avoid them if you can."

"When I shattered one of them to pieces, I noticed a very small red sphere which fell onto the ice and then burrowed into it, disappearing almost at once." The Amazon glanced at Idron with an expression of mute inquiry.

"And what conclusion do you draw from that?" Idron inquired.

The Amazon gave a grim smile. "There is a theory that low forms of life can exist in space, adapting themselves both to a vacuum and temperatures of absolute zero. I think those small red globules—or spores if you prefer—are the real Drexei."

Abna nodded. "So, they arrived on this world either by drifting down from space or possibly in some large meteorites since there are a few big craters here. Whenever any intruders land, they somehow gather that frozen atmosphere around themselves in the shape of those creatures we saw."

* * * *

An hour later, the Crusaders made their way back to where the *Ultra* stood waiting. This time only Credar accompanied them. His lined features were solemn as he stood with them at the bottom of the ladder. "I fear you are heading into grave danger in your attempt to help us. It is unfortunate we can tell you so little of what you want to know but living here as we do, shut off from the outside, we have little knowledge of events taking place beyond our world."

"You've already provided us with some information," the Amazon said quietly. "The rest we shall have to find out for ourselves."

"Will you return?" Credar asked.

"Perhaps," Abna replied. "Much will depend on what we discover out there. Those spaceships we saw did not just disappear. My guess is they made for that other world. If that is so, we'll find them."

"And when you do? You cannot fight an entire planet. Quite frankly, I fear for the outcome of whatever you try to do."

"There's no need to worry about us," Viona declared stoutly. "In our voyaging through the galaxy we've come across a number of races who thought they could kill us and destroy the *Ultra* but, as you see, we are still here and they are not."

"Well said, Viona," Abna responded. He turned to face Credar. "How do we get back to the surface?"

Credar smiled but there was a serious cast to his expression. "Just return on board your vessel. We will do the rest. Once you are back on the surface, your engines will again work perfectly."

One after the other, the Crusaders climbed through the airlock, the ladder following them. They had a brief glimpse of the Xendorian standing a short distance away. Then the airlock door closed, and they made their way back to the control room, taking their usual seats before the vast hemisphere of the instrument panel.

No one spoke until they were all seated, then the Amazon said, "I was hoping for more from these people but either they know nothing more—or they're deliberately keeping something from us."

"Why should they do that?" Mexone queried. "They seemed not only friendly but quite open with their answers."

The Amazon's lips twisted into a grim smile. "Perhaps it's just my suspicious mind but, apart from the four of you, I trust no one."

Before she could elaborate further, there was a slight shudder and the next moment the *Ultra* was rising slowly from Xendor, its upward velocity increasing incrementally as they ascended towards the distant curvature of the enclosing rock. The world fell away below them. Then they reached the outer shell.

In spite of the knowledge that they were quite safe, Thania winced as they approached the rock. Then they were, once again, inside the rock and still rising slowly. How long the strange transition through the solid stone lasted, it was difficult to tell. The idea that every nanosecond the electrons of the atoms of the rock were being halted in their orbits to enable them to traverse this thick outer shell was one she could not understand fully in spite of the tremendous scientific knowledge which had been placed in her mind when she had become a Crusader.

At last, however, they emerged onto the planetary surface—only to find the *Ultra* completely surrounded by almost a hundred of the ice creatures! Thania uttered a faint cry of alarm as she saw them crowding forward.

"There's absolutely no need for panic," The Amazon told her evenly. "They cannot penetrate the hull of this vessel. We are quite secure."

"I wouldn't be too sure of that," Viona called loudly. "It seems they can still absorb heat from anything they touch with those tentacles. The temperature in here is beginning to go down—and rapidly."

Swiftly, Abna's hand moved, closing the switch in front of him and transferring the power to the atomic engines. With a smooth motion, the *Ultra* slid forward, rising as it did so. The surface of the planet dropped away as the spaceship lifted above the tall peaks of the mountains and headed into deep space.

But if the Crusaders thought they had freed themselves from the danger, they were soon proved wrong. It was Mexone who cried, "Those creatures are still there. They're clinging like glue to the outer hull, hundreds of them!"

Through the observation windows they could make out the grossly distorted shapes covering almost the entire surface of the hull.

"Quite clearly there's nothing we can do to shake them off," Abna said. "We'll have to think of something else—and quickly or they'll drain all of the heat from the ship. Being in space won't kill them since they live on that planet in an absolute vacuum."

By now, the temperature inside the control room had dropped to the point that they were all shivering with the cold.

It was the Amazon who made the first suggestion. "Perhaps if we were to pass a powerful electric current through the outer shell that might be sufficient to dislodge them."

"It's certainly worth a try," Abna conceded.

"But won't we all be electrocuted?" Thania asked.

The Amazon shook her blonde head. "No, we'll be quite safe. There's an insulating shield inside the hull. Fortunately I had that put in place just in case we ran into any violent electrical storms. Such things have been known in the galaxy, sometimes several light years in diameter."

She moved quickly towards a small instrument bank at the end of the console, made a deft adjustment and then flicked down a switch. Outside, the entire length of the *Ultra* suddenly blazed with flickering sparks that danced among the creatures clinging to the metal.

CHAPTER III

TENSELY, the Amazon waited, allowing the tremendous discharge to continue for several minutes. Then she flicked off the switch. "Has anything happened out there?" she called.

Viona moved to the nearest window and threw a quick glance along the hull in both directions. Without turning her head, she replied, "It doesn't seem to have had any effect on them, mother. They're still there and apparently unharmed."

"This is certainly the oddest life-form I've ever come across," the Amazon muttered as she returned to the main console. "Creatures that can survive at absolute zero, in a vacuum, and immune to a sustained electrical shock of that magnitude."

"What's the internal temperature now, Viona?" Abna called in a voice filled with concern.

"Minus seven degrees and still falling," Viona answered.

The Amazon said: "I think we'd better get back into our protective suits. We should be able to maintain our body heat in them for a time while we think of something to destroy these things."

Putting the controls on automatic, Abna donned his suit, helping the others with theirs before going back to the console. It was now almost impossible to see through the wide viewing screen. Virtually every square inch was covered by the creatures.

Somehow, the Amazon forced herself to think clearly and coherently. This was a danger they had not foreseen and she was forced to admit she could think of no answer to their dilemma. They had destroyed these beings by means of sheer brute force but that was out of the question now. Even if they went outside the ship, the task of shattering the creatures to bits would place all of them in danger from those whip-like tentacles.

"There has to be an answer somewhere if we can only think of it," she said sharply. "I refuse to believe that the greatest scientific brains of the Solar System can be defeated by these monsters."

"And don't forget that other race which comes here to mine those deposits," Mexone said. "My guess is they have some means of controlling them otherwise they would be attacked on the surface and their vessels covered with them."

"Perhaps if I were to try to get into their minds, I might be able to do something," Abna suggested, "unless they are completely mindless creatures."

"Then try it." There was a note of urgency in the Amazon's voice. "If we don't do something quickly, the temperature inside the ship will be the same as that void out there—absolute zero. And our suits won't keep us warm forever."

Leaning forward a little over the control console, Abna composed himself. His handsome features were set like stone in concentration.

He remained thus for several minutes, then pulled himself together and shook his head. "It's no use, Vi. Either they have no minds at all, or there is some shield around them which even I cannot penetrate."

At this news, the Crusaders looked about them, seeking some means of ridding themselves of the creatures now covering the *Ultra*. Sitting beside Abna, the Amazon racked her brains searching through her extensive scientific knowledge. By now, frost was beginning to form on the interior of the walls and the controls. With the temperature still falling, they knew they had to do something, or it would not be long before they froze to death.

Even the small generators that supplied heat to their suits would soon fail and that would be the end of them. As the thought passed through her mind, the Amazon leapt up from her seat. "We may have one chance," she declared. "I don't know if it will work but it's worth taking the risk."

Abna stared up at her. "Just what do you have in mind, Vi?"

"These creatures are absorbing the heat from inside the *Ultra*. But there must be a limit to the amount of heat they can take in before they start to melt. After all, they're only made up of solidified atmospheric gases. Whatever mechanism there is in their bodies which prevents this melting from happening, if we can overload it to the point where they can no longer function properly—"

Abna nodded. "We know nothing of their metabolism but it's the only chance we have. I suggest we try it."

"But how do we do it?" Thania put in. "And will the hull of the *Ultra* withstand all that heat?"

Smiling grimly, the Amazon crossed to a bank of switches on the far wall. To Thania, she said, "The hull of this spaceship has been designed to survive impacts from meteorites and nuclear weapons. All I have to do is divert some of the heat from the engines into the outer walls. It will have to be done extremely carefully, of course."

Studying the switches for a few moments, she then flicked down three in quick succession. There was a slight change in their forward velocity but nothing else was apparent.

A moment later, she called, "Let me know if anything is happening."

Both Viona and Thania ran to the windows and a moment later, Mexone joined them. A minute dragged by—and then another. Her every sense geared to the task in hand, the Amazon manipulated the switches in front of her. It was going to be a very delicate balance between the power she needed to drain from the engines and that necessary to destroy the enemy outside.

Then Viona let out a sudden yell. "They're beginning to melt and disappear. You've done it!"

It was true. All along the great length of the *Ultra* the creatures were falling in upon themselves, evaporating into the vast emptiness. Large areas of metal appeared where they had earlier been covered in white. Slowly, the last of the creatures steamed and then vaporized. Within a comparatively short while, the huge ship was clear of hem and it was possible to see through the visiscreen.

Behind them, on the rear viewer, the planet they had left was now lost among the multitude of stars, so great had been their forward velocity while they had been immersed in the problem of ridding themselves of their attackers. Checking the temperature gauge, the Amazon saw that it was now rising slowly towards its normal limits. Smoothly, she operated the switches, stopping the power to the hull.

Operating the forward thrusts, Abna slowed the huge vessel before turning it in a wide arc. "We're now quite a distance from that solar system," he said, "But it shouldn't be too difficult to pick out that sun again. I doubt if there are any others like it in this region of the Milky Way."

Ten minutes later they spotted the sun almost dead ahead.

"What do you intend doing now, Vi?" he asked. "Are you still determined to investigate the odd behavior of that sun?"

"I'm more determined than ever now," the Amazon replied firmly. "But first, I'd like to take a look at the other world in this system. If it is the home of that race which is attacking Xendor and stealing their frozen atmosphere and rocks I want to do something about it."

"You mean go in there with all guns blazing?" Thania asked, her face alive with anticipation.

"Not exactly." The Amazon admonished gently. "Whoever they are, they clearly believe they're the dominant race there and they'll undoubtedly put up a fight. I just want to be ready for them if they do."

"Then the best thing to do would be to remain some distance from it and scan it with the ultra-telescope," Abna said. "That should give us some useful information without drawing us into conflict with them."

"Those are my feelings entirely," the Amazon concurred.

While the ever-cautious Mexone kept a sharp lookout for any of the enemy vessels, Abna reduced their velocity still further until they were a mere forty million miles from the planet. Approaching it from space, much of the surface was in shadow, only a thin sliver of the sunlit side being visible.

"Now let's see what the ultra-telescope can tell us." The Amazon seated herself behind the controls. A flick of a switch and the image appeared on the vast visiscreen. It showed a pale pink crescent with no visible markings. The dark side also revealed no information.

The image enlarged swiftly as the Amazon adjusted the controls. Soon it almost filled the entire area of the screen. Even then, the portion of it which was illuminated by the strange sun was completely featureless. Sitting back in her seat, the Amazon pursed her lips in contemplative silence.

After a few moments, she remarked, "From what little I can see, that planet reminds me strongly of Venus. Evidently, it's completely covered by a thick atmosphere so we can see no surface details. Before we go any further, I think we should get a spectroscopic picture of that atmosphere."

"And you think this planet may be similar to Venus?" Viona came to peer closely at the image.

The Amazon said nothing but continued to study the image intently. Then she said, "Obviously with all that cloud cover, we're going to get no information from the ultra-telescope. We can, however, try the long-distance radar. Whatever is in that atmosphere that will pass through it easily and give us a picture of the surface—a kind of map we can study."

Focusing the deep-space radar on the distant planet, they waited for the results to come in. Penetrating the thick layer of gases covering the night side of the world, the radar pulses swept across the hidden surface in a series of narrow, overlapping bands, slowly building up a picture of the terrain beneath.

Half an hour later the radar had made a complete sweep of the entire hemisphere, showing three large continents and two oceans. The land masses appeared mountainous with long, winding narrow valleys. There was also evidence of an ice cap at one of the poles but none at the other.

Abna spotted the latter immediately. "Whether that is water or carbon dioxide ice, it does tell us that the temperature on that world should be bearable. That is almost certainly due to the much lower temperature of the luminary. I would also guess that this planet, like Mercury in our own solar system, always turns the same hemisphere towards the sun. That means the day is as long as the year."

"Speaking of the luminary," Viona said, "there's something I've just noticed which I don't understand." She was standing beside one of the ports, staring out into space.

"And what might that be?" Abna asked, coming to stand beside her.

"That sun out there. Don't you see?"

The Amazon came over and joined them. After a moment, she said, "I don't see anything different about it. Those pulsations are continuing as before, and—"

She broke off sharply with a sudden intake of breath. "I see what you mean. That curious distortion of those pulsations we saw from out in space is much more noticeable now. Whatever it is, I can't explain it. Can you, Abna?"

Shrugging, Abna replied, "The only thing I can suggest is that there is some kind of interference affecting the light emitted from that sun. As to its cause, your guess is as good as mine."

The Amazon pondered that for a while then, always wanting to be doing something constructive, not wasting time on things to which they had no answer, she said, "Then if there's no indication of any spaceships in the vicinity, I think we should land at some suitable spot and take a look around. Once we get closer we can make final checks on the atmosphere and temperature."

The *Ultra* now flashed across the space between them and the cloud-covered planet. Soon, under Abna's deft handling, they were hovering less than a thousand miles above the atmosphere. In the weird sunlight, the disc varied endlessly from a pale pink to a deep crimson. On the wide panel above the controls, further details came in as more instruments on board the vessel fed in their data.

The temperature varied between twenty degrees at the equator to well below zero at the poles. Contrary to what they had thought, the atmosphere contained a large proportion of oxygen, being more Earth-like than they had expected. There were, however, a number of large, active volcanoes, several of which had been picked up earlier by the radar scan.

"Conditions down there appear to be better than we originally thought, Vi," Abna remarked. "We should be able to land without too much trouble. The humidity is quite high but I think we can handle that without too many problems."

"Then let's do it," the Amazon said briskly. "I want to see just what lies beneath this thick atmosphere. We've wasted enough time."

"And if this is the world where those spacecraft came from?" Viona said, adding a word of caution.

"Then if they are a warlike race, I'm sure we can give a good account of ourselves. After all, the major part of our mission through the galaxy is to prevent such people imposing their will on other peaceful races."

Turning the nose of the *Ultra* towards the planet, they speared down into the dense atmosphere. To combat the inevitable friction, Abna cut the velocity still further. Outside, there was nothing to be seen. The sunlight was completely blotted out. Deeper and deeper they went and still there was no sign of a clearance beyond the ports.

"How far are we above the surface?" the Amazon asked sharply. "Surely this thick cloud layer doesn't extend all the way down. We won't discover much walking through a dense fog."

"We're still forty thousand feet above the ground," Abna answered. "There's plenty of room in which to maneuver. The radar will give us sufficient of warning of any high mountains in the area."

"I'll switch on the long-range radio—see if we can pick up anything with that," Viona said. The radio, however, remained silent except for the usual crackle of static. After a few moments, she added, "There's nothing coming through on any of the wavelengths. If there is anyone living down there, they're either of a low intelligence or they use some other means of communication."

At thirty thousand feet, the cloud around them began to thin and vague details appeared. These became clearer as the *Ultra* descended still further. They were skimming over a large ocean, its sullen surface a dark gray in the eternal twilight. Vast in extent, it seemed to stretch forever with no end in sight.

Occasionally, they discerned huge aquatic shapes, their outlines unfamiliar to any of the Crusaders.

Then a dark smudge appeared on the horizon. There was a wide sandy beach and then tall trees appeared below them. The Amazon eyed them critically as they flew over them, finally saying, "This looks like a primal jungle world, rather like Earth some five hundred million years ago. It's highly unlikely we'll find any intelligent life here."

"Still, it's worth a look." Abna remarked. "If those aliens we spotted didn't come from this planet—where did they come from? As far as we know, this is the only other planet orbiting this sun."

"Then I suggest we land in the first suitable space we can find. From the look of that jungle down there, it won't be easy. It seems to cover the entire land mass."

Viona, standing at the visiscreen, suddenly pointed. "There seems to be an open space over there. It looks big enough for us to land."

* * * *

The landing was difficult, but Abna had skillfully put the *Ultra* down under worse conditions as these and ten minutes later, skimming above the gigantic trees, he lowered the spaceship down in the wide glade Viona had indicated. Huge as the *Ultra* was, the massive trees towered above it. Gigantic cycads flourished everywhere. Trailing fern-like growths clambered among the trees.

Switching off the engines, Abna said, "The first thing to do is check that atmosphere outside. The temperature is somewhat higher than on Earth, possibly due to a greenhouse effect. I also think the humidity will be a slight problem but not something we can't overcome."

While he had been speaking, the Amazon and Mexone had checked the readings that came in from the instruments on board. Finally, the full picture of the external environment emerged. Radioactivity was well below the danger limit. The oxygen content and gravity were also above Earth normal but overall the conditions seemed suitable for them to go outside without any protective clothing.

Ever impatient to be doing something positive, the Amazon was the first to climb down the ladder onto the surface. For a moment, she stood listening to the sounds of the nearby jungle. The dull gray-pink of the sky was depressing but she shrugged the sensation away. In certain respects, the vista resembled that of Thoron, the planet circling the seetee sun they had visited on the rim of the galaxy. But there were differences.

This world was clearly a much younger one, like Earth in the age of the dinosaurs and her hand went instinctively to the protonic blaster at her hip as the thought crossed her mind.

Dropping down beside her, Viona gazed around the clearing with an expression of awe on her youthful face. "I can't wait to investigate that jungle out there. Do you think there could be people like us around?"

"I doubt that very much," her mother replied. "On similar planets evolution usually follows approximately the same pattern. On Earth, for example, life started in the oceans before there was a migration onto the land. The large reptiles came and it was hundreds of millions of years later before anything like human beings evolved."

Mexone had overheard her remark. He said quietly, "Then you don't think those aliens we saw are native to this world?"

"No. Quite frankly, I don't. Whoever they are, it's clear their scientific status is not much dissimilar to our own. This world appears to be too young for a highly developed and intelligent creature to have put in an appearance in the usual scheme of things. Apart from that—"

She stopped in mid-sentence as a sound like the trump of doom reached them from somewhere in the depths of the steaming jungle. Something truly massive crashed through the trees and it was clearly heading in their direction.

"Evidently our arrival here has not gone unnoticed," Abna said, drawing his own weapon.

The next moment a great scaled head thrust through the upper branches of the trees a couple of hundred yards away. It was followed by a huge, armored body. The creature stood upright on two thickly muscled legs ending in long claws.

"My God, what is that thing?" There was a faint note of terror in Thania's voice,

"It's a dinosaur of some kind," the Amazon said, "rather like the Tyrannosaurus Rex which once inhabited Earth but more than twice as large. But if it thinks it's going to have us for breakfast, it's wrong."

Swiftly, she aimed the protonic blaster at the creature's head as it came thundering in their direction. A huge chunk of scaly flesh exploded from the dinosaur's head. A second blast hit it full in the armored chest. A shrill hissing scream echoed across the jungle. For a second, the monster reared up on its massive hind legs. The huge mouth, lined with two-foot-long teeth gaped open,

Its forward momentum carried it several yards into the clearing before it collapsed onto the mud. Even though the last shot had hit its vital organs, it still jerked and twisted in its death throes before finally lying still.

Still maintaining her grip on the weapon, the Amazon went cautiously forward.

Slowly, the others followed. Thania's face still bore an expression of awe and apprehension. Never before had she imagined such a huge creature. To her, it was like something out of a nightmare.

Finally, in a voice that quavered a little, she asked, "Do you think there are any more like this wandering around the jungle?"

"There are sure to be," Abna answered. "Such monstrous reptiles lived for millions of years on Earth before something wiped them out almost overnight The most widely held theory is that either a huge comet, or an asteroid, struck the Earth all those years ago, destroying much of the vegetation and other animals which provided them with food. It may also have caused a drastic change in the atmosphere making it impossible for them to survive."

"At least we know our weapons can kill them," Viona declared. Being totally without fear, she moved towards the jungle until the Amazon called her back.

"We don't intend to hunt them down just for the fun of it," she said reprovingly. "I've no doubt we'll meet up with more of them during our stay here and—"

"You mean to remain here for some time?" Abna glanced at her in surprise. "It's quite obvious this isn't the home world of that race we saw earlier. If there are any creatures even remotely humanoid on this planet, they'll be on the same cultural level as primitive cave men."

"I agree," The Amazon assented. "And I also realize that a highly advanced race that can build spaceships would not have evolved in the relatively short time there has been life here."

"Then why stay?"

"Because I have this feeling that there's something here, something important, and I intend to find it."

"Is that just feminine intuition, or based on some kind of scientific reasoning?" Abna asked.

"Don't belittle feminine intuition, Abna, it's got me out of a few tight comers in the past." Irritated a little by the remark, the Amazon adroitly changed the subject. "The situation is this. Much of the land mass appears to be covered by dense jungle and swamps. Clearly any survey is going to be long and tedious, so I suggest we divide our force. Abna—you take Thania in one of the pinnaces. Mexone and Viona will come with me through the jungle on foot. We'll meet back here in two hours."

"And what are we supposed to be looking for?" Thania asked.

The Amazon pursed her lips; then said, "Anything out of the ordinary, particularly any sign of humanoids. If we can contact them, we might just be able to learn something."

There followed a short while as the starboard pinnace was brought to the airlock ready for launching. Once everything was in readiness, Abna took the controls with Thania occupying the seat beside him. Seconds later, it took off, remaining in sight just beneath the overlying layers of thick cloud.

Once the vessel had disappeared, the Amazon closed the airlock with the small remote control; then turned to face the brooding green jungle. Despite their light clothing, they were sweating in the humidity. The thick clouds were like a weight pressing on their shoulders. Cautiously, they made their way around the massive bulk of the dead dinosaur. Where it had approached there was now a wide, open swathe where the huge trees had been smashed and flattened.

This they took, relieving them of the necessity of thrusting their way through the dense tangle of the undergrowth. Weird sounds occasionally echoed through the brooding stillness. Even the trees, twined with thick creepers oozed an air of menace. They had progressed almost a mile when they were forced to an abrupt halt. In front of them a wide rift prevented any further progress.

The ground fell away almost perpendicularly for several hundred feet towards a rocky bottom. There a narrow river rushed in a frothing torrent across the stony bed.

"It looks as though we can go no further this way." Mexone remarked. He walked cautiously to the edge and peered down.

The Amazon said nothing for a full minute, her keen gaze studying the lie of the land. Then she took the long, thin rope from her belt.

Her two companions stared at her in surprise. "You don't mean to use that to get across, do you?" Viona asked. "It's impossible."

"Nothing is impossible if you put your mind to it," the Amazon remarked. Making a secure loop at one end, she whirled it around her head and then released it, sending the rope snaking across the broad gap. The first attempt fell short. Undaunted, she tried again.

This time the loop caught around a tall spear of rock on the far side. Carefully, she pulled it taut, hauling on it with all her strength until she was certain the far end was anchored safely to the rock. Within moments, she had fastened the other end to a similar spur of rock.

"We go over one at a time," she said tautly. "I know it's risky but I don't intend to stand here and do nothing. I'll go first, then you Viona. You come last, Mexone."

Reaching the edge of the steep drop, the Amazon bent and leaned forward as far as she dared. Then she grasped the rope with both hands and gracefully swung herself out over the precipice. Hand over hand, she drew herself forward, not once looking down into the yawning chasm beneath her feet.

Viona and Mexone watched her progress breathlessly. The slender rope bent beneath the Amazon's weight, but it was incredibly strong and held her easily.

Through taut lips, Mexone said, "This is what I really call living dangerously, Viona. Trust your mother to come up with something like this."

By now, the Amazon had reached the middle of the canyon, suspended in midair with only the rope and her superb strength between her and a plummeting drop onto the sharply pointed rocks below. Now the test of strength was even harder since she had also to pull herself upward towards the far rim.

Slowly, a foot at a time, she drew herself forward. The only sound now was the eternal rushing of the water far below. Then, incredibly, she was across, pulling herself over the edge before standing and turning to wave Viona on.

Almost without pausing to consider the danger, the girl grasped the rope in her clenched fists and launched herself into empty space. Swinging her legs slightly from side to side, she managed to give herself a little extra impetus but even her muscles were beginning to ache with the strain by the time she was halfway across.

Like her mother, she knew better than to look down, or to even pause in the endless motion of swinging one hand in front of the other. Instinctively, she knew that if she stopped, she might dangle there forever, unable to continue moving.

Then a hand reached out, grasped her wrist and pulled her onto the rocky ledge where she rubbed her aching shoulders and glanced back to where Mexone was beginning the crossing.

Anxiously, she asked, "He'll be all right, won't he?"

"He'll make it. After all, he's a Cosmic Crusader like the rest of us."

They watched tensely as Mexone passed the halfway mark and commenced the long pull towards where they were standing. Then, when he was less than twenty feet from the end, Mexone's left hand missed the rope. Viona uttered a sharp cry of alarm as he hung there with one hand, desperately struggling to pull himself up with one arm in order to grasp the rope.

Without pausing to think, knowing only that he could hold on only for a matter of a few seconds, the Amazon flung herself forward. Hand over hand, she quickly made her way to where he dangled above the gorge.

"Wrap your legs around my waist," she called urgently.

"Don't be a fool, Amazon," he gasped hoarsely, "you can't—"

"Do as I say. Quickly!"

Mexone hesitated, then swung his legs forward, clasping them around the Amazon's slender waist, just as his other hand slipped from the rope.

Clenching her teeth, the Amazon braced herself as she took his additional weight on her arms. Steel muscles flexed beneath her tights as she slowly worked her way backwards. Slowly, a foot at a time, she drew herself along the rope.

She only knew she had made it when her shoulders touched the hard rock. Then Viona leaned down, grabbed Mexone's wrists and pulled him over the edge before leaning down and helping the Amazon.

Rubbing his aching wrists, Mexone said harshly, "That is an experience I would not like to do again."

"I'm afraid you may have to," the Amazon said. "I'm leaving the rope here. We may have to use it again on our way back—unless you can think of an easier way of crossing this chasm." She pulled him to his feet. "Now let us go forward and see what we can find."

In front of them, the massive trees gave no indication of any opening through them. Trailing creepers thicker than a man's arm looped and twined in all directions.

Even their knives proved of little value in hacking through the almost impenetrable undergrowth.

Wiping her brow, the Amazon paused and looked around her. "We won't get very far like this," she muttered finally. "The only thing we can do is burn a way through this vegetation."

From her belt, she took out the small welder and indicated the others were to do likewise. Swinging the brilliant flames in a sideways motion in front of them, they made slightly better progress. The welders sliced through the tough creepers with ease and much of the other impeding growth shriveled and turned into ash.

It was, however, hot work. By the time they had made their way through the growth for a hundred yards, the sweat was streaming down their faces, running into their eyes, making it difficult to see what they were doing. They worked in silence. It was too hot to think clearly, let alone talk.

Then the Amazon held up a restraining hand, bringing Viona and Mexone to an instant standstill. Directly ahead of them was a narrow opening in the jungle. Through it they saw a wide valley and down below them, a herd of gigantic animals moved slowly in a single line along the valley bottom. Viona emitted a sharp gasp of amazement.

"Those creatures are even bigger than that monster we killed," she exclaimed, scarcely able to believe her eyes.

The Amazon gave a brief nod. "Fortunately for us, they appear to be vegetarians and not flesh eaters like that other creature we met. I don't think we'll have any trouble with them but—"

She jerked up her head swiftly without finishing her sentence. They had been so engrossed in watching the movements of the herd below, they had forgotten that the air might also present a danger.

A series of harsh, raucous cries tore the silence into shreds, hammering at their ears. Three black shapes came swooping towards them. Huge leathery wings outspread, their gaping mouths showing rows of serrated teeth, they glided swiftly towards the Crusaders.

Balancing herself dexterously, the Amazon brought up her blaster. Her first shot missed as her target swerved but the second tore one of the wings from its body. The creature lurched drunkenly and then spiraled down towards the valley. Mexone and Viona, although taken by surprise by the suddenness of the attack, immediately swung into action.

A bolt from Viona's weapon sent another monster crashing to the ground, its head hanging limply on its neck. The third, however, abruptly twisted out of the air just above Mexone.

A huge wing caught Mexone on the shoulder and strong as he was, it knocked him to the ground and moments later, the creature had straddled him, the vicious beaked mouth reaching for his face.

Without a single thought for her own safety, Viona leapt forward. Not daring to use the blaster for fear of hitting her husband, she dropped the weapon and clamped both of her hands around the beaked mouth. The muscles in her arms stood out as she pulled back with all of her strength, dragging the threshing creature off Mexone's prostrate body. Bracing herself, she swung round, hauling the monster off its feet. With a deft pivot, she slammed it hard against the trunk of a giant tree.

There was the crack of thin bones. The attacker hung there for a moment, then slid inertly to the ground. Straightening up, Viona bent and retrieved her weapon, holding it in readiness for any further attack. For the moment, however, there appeared to be nothing. The huge, long-necked creatures in the valley were grazing peacefully, clearly oblivious to their presence.

Extending a hand, Viona pulled Mexone to his feet. Apart from a few bruises, he seemed little the worse for his recent encounter.

"It would seem," the Amazon said after a momentary pause, "that we've stumbled upon a world full of these prehistoric monsters. Whether there are any humanoids here is doubtful if the history of Earth is anything to go by. There, primitive man didn't appear for several hundred million years after the last of the reptiles died out."

"And there's another point to consider," Mexone pointed out. "Even if there are, how are we going to communicate with them? I presume that would be your intention, Amazon."

"That's true, mother," Viona said. "The other races we've met with in the past did, at least, have a modicum of intelligence to allow Abna to either impress English into their minds—or absorb enough of their language to get by. From what I've seen of this world, if there are any human-like creatures around, they'll be on a level of intelligence only just above the animals."

"I've already considered that possibility," the Amazon replied. "First we have to find them—if they exist."

"And then—?" Viona asked.

Smiling a little, the Amazon said, "Then we may have to resort to some form of sign language. Now I suggest we move on. We'll discover nothing simply standing here talking. Let's see what's on the other side of that valley."

Scrambling down the steep slope, they reached the bottom and set out through the waist high grass. Some distance away, the huge creatures lumbered slowly past them. As the Amazon had surmised, they paid no attention to the Crusaders. Occasionally, one would turn its head to stare down at them and then resume eating the leaves from the highest branches of the nearby trees.

The far side of the valley proved to be more difficult to ascend than they had anticipated. It was strewn with large boulders, cracked by deep gullies that hampered every movement. In addition, the overbearing heat and humidity did little to help them.

Pausing halfway up the slope, Mexone wiped the streaming sweat from his eyes and face. "How much further do you intend to go, Amazon?" he asked throatily. "We've already been on the move for almost an hour. If Abna hasn't ran into trouble, he'll be back at the *Ultra* long before we get there."

"If we don't find anything but more jungle at the top there, we'll turn back," the Amazon replied. "In any event I can always contact him with my wrist radio."

Pushing on with a grim purpose, she led them the rest of the way, pausing as she reached the crest. Stepping up beside her, Viona noticed the look of surprise on the Amazon's face as she stared straight ahead.

A high hillside towered over a level stretch of ground. Some distance away, a number of large circular openings were visible in the rock. The trio eyed them speculatively. Finally, Viona said quietly, "Those openings seem to have been artificially made—but why and who by?"

"Evidently someone lives there." The Amazon pointed towards the far side of the area. "Notice that pile of animal bones. I'd say we've found a small community of cave dwellers."

Mexone nodded in agreement. "Clearly those caves are the only places of safety from the huge beasts roaming this world. If they lived in the jungle they would soon be easy meat for such creatures."

"Do you think we should make contact with them?" Viona asked. "Even if they are warlike, our weapons will be sufficient to protect us."

"Very well, we'll—"

A sudden thunderous roar interrupted the Amazon. At first, she thought it was another of the ferocious dinosaurs that had somehow picked up their scent. Then she realized the sound came from almost directly above their heads and it was growing louder with every passing second.

"Get back into those trees yonder," the Amazon pointed urgently, knowing that her warning could not be heard above the clamoring thunder of a descending spaceship.

* * * *

Keeping well beneath the thick cloud layer, Abna sent the small pinnace hurtling across the green carpet of jungle. Beside him, Thania watched the ground below with a mixture of awe and scientific curiosity. This was something that did not exist on her home world, something she had never imagined before.

Inwardly, she had to admit that the sight of that monstrous animal which had attacked them had terrified her. Even the fact that the protonic blasters had killed it almost instantly had failed to subdue her fears entirely. At least, she thought, she was completely safe here, high above those trees and with Abna, a highly skilled pilot, at the controls.

They had been flying for almost five minutes before she asked, "Does the Amazon really believe she'll find something important on this world? I mean, there's nothing but jungle and those huge monsters down there. If she hopes to find an answer to the peculiar behavior of this sun, surely it won't be here."

Abna adjusted the controls slightly as the radar showed the presence of higher ground ahead. Without taking his eyes off the instruments, he said, "She sometimes gets these strange notions, Thania, often without any real scientific evidence to back them up."

Smiling slightly, he added, "The thing is that quite often she's been proved right."

"Well, I don't see anything out of the ordinary down there—just a monotonous stretch of green and—"

She broke off sharply as the pinnace suddenly rocked as if struck by an invisible fist. "What's happening?" Somehow, she got the words out.

"I'm not sure. We've been hit by an atmospheric shock wave—a big one." For several minutes the pinnace bounced up and down as Abna fought with the controls. Gradually, he brought it onto a more even keel. Steadying herself once she had got over the shock, Thania peered through the window, struggling to make out what could have caused the blast. The gray-pink clouds stretched away as far as she could see and there was nothing there that might have caused the disturbance in the atmosphere.

Then, in front of them, some distance away, the clouds assumed an angry red color that pulsed in an odd manner. Clutching tightly at the control panel, Thania clenched her fingers and held on as the small craft again spun temporarily out of control.

The radar instrument uttered a loud, warning bleep. "That red glow dead ahead." Abna pointed.

"What is it?"

"There must be a volcano down there! Hold on tight. We've got to change course quickly and get away from it."

Gritting his teeth, Abna used all his tremendous strength to control the pinnace, and take them higher, turning the vessel sharply to the right through a tight arc. Moments later, they were inside the thick cloud and now they had no view of the outside world. More tremendous jolts came. The slender craft slid sideways as Abna fed more power to the atomic engines. The steep climb continued and now they faced a new danger.

A series of hammering impacts sounded against the hull. Rocks, ejected with high velocities from the erupting volcano struck them on all sides. The red glare outside gave their features a ghastly look. And there was more. A thick layer of volcanic dust smeared the observation window so that now Abna had to rely solely on the radar.

It was impossible for Thania to estimate how long the climb took for them to rise above the boiling cloud of ash and stones. The uprush of superheated air from the volcano helped to lift them but it continued to rock them violently from side to side.

Bobbing like a cork on water, the pinnace gradually climbed still higher. Each individual second dragged itself out into an eternity of sound and jolting motion. Then, gradually, the noise lessened. The shuddering impacts of flying rocks diminished and then ceased. They had reached the uppermost layer of the dense atmosphere. A moment later they were out in space with the glittering stars shining all around them.

Below them, a circle of angry red marked the position of the volcano. Setting the controls on automatic, Abna leaned back in his seat and let his pent-up breath go in a long exhalation. The effort of fighting against that titanic eruption had taken a lot out of him.

Finally, he forced a reassuring grin. "That is one experience I wouldn't like to go through again. I'm sorry, Thania—it was my fault entirely. I really should have foreseen it. There are plenty of volcanoes on my home-world of Jupiter and they were apparently common on Earth hundreds of millions of years ago."

"I can hardly imagine anything more terrifying," Thania sat on the edge of her seat. Slowly, she forced her tensed muscles to relax.

"Of course," Abna nodded. "You've never seen one before. Not that you saw much of this one through that dense cloud. This world is going through its early stages of evolution. Inevitably, there are weak spots in its surface and when the pressure inside its molten core becomes too great, it forces tremendous amounts of molten rock into the air with explosive violence. Great rivers of lava flow down the sides, destroying everything in their path."

He nodded briefly as he gave the instruments a quick glance. "Fortunately, the hull of this vessel is strong enough to have sustained little damage from those rocks otherwise we would have been in serious trouble. Now we know where that volcano is, however, we can go down again and continue our survey."

Plunging back into the atmosphere, they descended once more to the lower levels avoiding the area around the eruption. Here the terrain differed somewhat from that which they had seen earlier. It was mostly an area of flat swampland and a wide sluggish river inhabited by large groups of lumbering creatures. Among these, however, were other animals, similar in shape to the huge dinosaur they had killed—but much smaller. Clearly these were predators— swift-moving carnivores.

Thania watched with an expression of mingled horror and distaste as they attacked their enormous prey. Three or four of them would fling themselves onto the enormous hides, clinging there with sharp claws. In this manner, it was not long before they brought down one of the huge beasts.

"Is this what it was really like on the Amazon's world half a billion of years ago?" she asked in a whisper.

"I'm afraid it was," Abna acknowledged solemnly. "In those times, and as it is now on this planet, it's a case of kill or be killed."

They flew on, over the wide river, towards a massive escarpment that now dominated the skyline ahead of them. Even while they were still some distance from it, both of the Crusaders noticed something peculiar about the approaching rock formation.

There seemed to be an odd symmetry about the high, sheer surface that made it stand out from anything else they had previously seen. Smoothly, Abna slowed the craft until they were scarcely moving.

"This is something I'd never have expected to find here," he muttered with a puzzled frown. "All of those massive carvings, huge pillars, and those huge doors set in the exact center of that cliff face. The nearest thing I can compare it with are the huge temples built on Earth by the Ancient Egyptians and Sumerians—and that was only about five thousand years ago."

Flicking a sequence of switches, he set the pinnace down on the flat ground some three hundred yards from the cliff, shutting off the atomic drive.

As they climbed down onto the planetary surface, Thania asked, "Why would you not expect to find this? After all, they're just carvings although admittedly on a very large scale."

"Because unless we're very much mistaken about this world, those could never have been made by the primitive kind of people we would expect to find under these conditions. This is a primal planet. Such worlds always evolve in a similar way.

"First there are small organisms in the sea which, over a few million years eventually emerge onto the land. After a few more hundreds of million of years they've evolved into these massive reptiles and only much later do intelligent creatures come into existence. The only explanation I can find for what we're now seeing is that it was made by that race whose spacecraft we saw leaving Xendor."

Slowly, keeping a sharp watch for any movement, they walked towards the massive doors. Two great stone pillars, one on each side, towered above them. Abna's puzzlement increased as he ran his gaze over them. They were perfectly smooth and had obviously been carved out of the solid rock.

Utterly dwarfed by them, the Crusaders stood before the gates. There was no visible means of entry. Stepping forward, Abna ran his hand over the surface. "It seems to be some kind of metal," he said at last. "And whoever built them didn't mean anyone to get inside."

"You think this may be what the Amazon is looking for? She said she believed there was something important on this world."

Taking out his blaster, Abna stood back a little way, aiming the weapon at the almost invisible join between the doors. Taking careful aim, he pressed the stud. The almost invisible beam of pure energy struck the join between the doors. He kept the beam on for a full two minutes; then switched it off.

"It's not having any effect," Thania said in a surprised tone.

Without answering, Abna took the small welder from his belt and tried that—but with the same result. Even the intense heat made no impression on the metal.

Shaking his head, he replaced the welder. "It's no use. Whatever those doors are made of, nothing we have with us can open them."

"But surely there must be a way of opening them?" Thania protested. "Doors without any keyhole or handle don't make any sense."

"We must remember that, at the moment; we don't know just how advanced this race is. It's quite possible these doors can only be opened electronically. They may even be opened just by one of these aliens speaking certain words. At present, we're completely in the dark."

"So, we're unable to do anything?"

"I'm afraid so. We'll have to wait until we get back to the *Ultra*. Perhaps the Amazon may have some ideas."

* * * *

Crouched down among the trees, the other three Crusaders watched as the great shape of the spaceship appeared out of the cloud layer and lowered itself slowly onto the ground some three hundred yards away. The Amazon's first thought that it was the *Ultra* was immediately dismissed from her mind.

This craft did not have the sleek lines of the *Ultra*. Ugly, sharply-angled protuberances jutted from the sides. Some appeared to be observation ports while the others were clearly armaments. A moment later, the engines were cut off and silence once again enveloped the clearing.

Parting the thick tangle of undergrowth in front of her, Viona said softly, "Why do you reckon they've landed here? Clearly there's some purpose behind it."

"My guess is they've come to speak with the natives," the Amazon answered grimly. "If the inhabitants of this planet are cave dwellers as I believe, they'll probably regard this race as gods come to visit them from the sky. Whatever it is these aliens want, you can be sure they'll be obeyed without question."

Frowning, Mexone whispered, "Yet I can't imagine what a highly advanced race could possibly want from such primitive people unless they take them away as slaves as those others from Andromeda did on Thoron."

"Well, it seems we're about to find out," the Amazon replied.

An airlock slid open halfway up the side of the alien spaceship and a long ladder appeared, extending towards the ground. Ten seconds later, four figures came out of the airlock and slowly descended the ladder.

Thin and gaunt, their hairless heads bore short antennae on either side in place of ears and their slanted eyes appeared to have no pupil. The characteristic that marked them out from any humanoids the Crusaders had encountered before were the four arms, two linked to each sloping shoulder.

"They look almost like overgrown insects," Mexone said in a low murmur.

The Amazon said nothing, watching closely as the leader advanced a couple of paces and then took a slender metallic instrument from his belt. Placing it to his lips, he blew three piercing notes. Scarcely had the shrill sounds died away than there was movement inside the caves.

The creatures that emerged were clearly only on a slightly higher level than apes although they walked upright, their long hairy arms almost touching the ground. Moving like automatons, they stood in a huddled group, their wide eyes beneath bulging brows fixed on the four aliens.

One of them, taller and more muscular than the others, moved forward at a gesture from the alien who took something from the belt around his waist.

Narrowing her eyes, the Amazon tried to make out what the object was. Even in the dull gloom, it sparkled with a multitude of colors. Reaching forward, the alien placed it against the cave man's forehead. When he drew back his hand, the object remained there as if glued to the skin.

"What's he doing?" Viona murmured softly.

Equally quietly, the Amazon said, "My guess is that he's somehow communicating with that aboriginal through that crystal. It must be some kind of thought transference device."

"If you're right, it would seem we're up against a race that is as scientifically advanced as we are," Mexone muttered.

"Father is capable of doing the same without the use of a crystal," Viona reminded him. Still keeping her head down, she edged forward a little way to get a better view.

The mental communication between the two lasted for several minutes. Then the alien removed the crystal and replaced it in his belt, evidently satisfied with the result. Turning, he made his way back up the ladder, followed by his three companions. As if this had happened before and the aboriginals knew what to expect, they drew back towards the caves.

The airlock slid shut behind the aliens and a couple of minutes later, with a thunderous roar of its exhaust, the spacecraft lifted off and vanished into the overhead murk.

Slowly, the deafening roar diminished until it was gone altogether. Getting lithely to her feet, the Amazon motioned to the others to follow her. "I think we should see if we can get anything out of these natives now that their masters have gone," she said.

"And if they recognize we're not the same as those others and decide to attack us?" Mexone queried. "Do we use our blasters?"

"Only as a last resort. Even if we have to use sign language, we may learn something about this other race. Somehow, I don't think they are indigenous to this world. We saw no sign of towns or cities to indicate these two different races live side-by-side."

The three of them stepped out of the trees onto the level ground. Instantly, all of the cave dwellers turned. Then the leader moved towards them, pausing in front of the Amazon who deliberately kept her hands away from the weapon in her belt. Baring his teeth in an almost bestial grimace, the cave man began stamping his feet as if acting out some strange ritualistic dance. Uttering a series of unintelligible grunts, urged on by shrill screeches from the others, he clenched his fists and hammered a rapid tattoo against his chest.

Without turning her head, the Amazon said, "They recognize that we're different from those others. They probably think we come from some other tribe. There are giant apes on Earth who act like this whenever others intrude upon their territory."

"So what does all this mean?" Mexone asked.

"I think he believes his position as head of this group is being threatened. My guess is that he's challenging me to a contest of strength."

"And if you refuse?" Viona asked.

"Then we either run away with our tails between our legs or they'll attack us."

Before she could say anything more, the cave man ceased his incessant tattoo. Towering at least two feet over her, he uttered a cavernous roar and leapt forward. Clamping his great hairy arms around the Amazon, he pinned her arms to her sides.

For a moment, taken completely by surprise, she remained immobile. Huge muscles stood out beneath the hairy skin of the aboriginal's great arms as he squeezed with all of his strength. Then, sucking in a deep breath, the Amazon exerted her own superhuman strength. Tightening her muscles, she gave a mighty heave.

For a moment, she thought it was not enough. The aboriginal was stronger than most of the adversaries she had met. Then his hold broke. Momentarily, he staggered off balance.

Before he could recover, the Amazon bent slightly, getting her hands beneath him. Straightening up almost effortlessly, she held his great bulk over her head and then threw him with all of her strength across the ground. He hit the hard-packed earth hard and rolled over several times before lurching to his feet.

The impact had stunned him, but he was still not out of the fight. Some sense of pride brought him forward once more. This time, he was more wary. Clearly, he had never expected a slim woman to possess more strength than himself. Grunting loudly, he bared his teeth again in a vicious snarl. Then he lowered his head and lunged towards the Amazon, his arms spread wide.

Standing balanced on her feet, the Amazon stood ready. It was evident he intended to grab her around the waist and throw her backward, off balance, hoping to pin her to the ground beneath his enormous bulk. At the very last moment, the Amazon skipped to one side. Her right hand lashed out and clamped around the other's wrist.

Whirling, she spun him round and then slammed him down hard onto the ground. Kneeling on his spine, she pulled both of his arms back. Steel-hard fingers that could crush bones to pulp, held him helpless. After holding him there for a minute, she released him and stood up. For a few seconds, the cave man lay there with all of the fight knocked out of him. Then, thrusting himself upright, he hesitated for a moment, then turned and shambled off towards the jungle.

"Where is he going?" Viona inquired.

Flexing her shapely shoulders, the Amazon replied, "He's been beaten and now he's no longer leader of these people. He'll either remain alone in the jungle or find another group and challenge its leader."

Pointing towards the caves, Mexone said, "It would seem as though you've now been elected leader here, Amazon."

The rest of the tribe, men, women, and children came crowding around them. "It looks as though you're right, Mexone. If only I could communicate with them, I'm sure we could learn a lot."

"That won't be easy," Viona interposed. "Their language seems to be nothing more than a series of grunts. Perhaps even Father could make nothing of it."

"Even that alien had to use some kind of thought gizmo to communicate with the leader," Mexone said.

"Then I'll try sign language. Firstly, I'd like to know if these people have any idea where these aliens come from." She glanced at her wrist chronometer. "And we haven't much time. We're not going to make it back to the *Ultra* in the time I asked Abna to meet us there."

Using her hands, she made a rough shape of the spaceship which had landed a little while earlier, indicated herself and her companions and then pointed to the jungle, moving in a full circle to embrace every direction.

One of the men made quick motions with his hands; then pointed up towards the sky.

With a quick nod, the Amazon said, "I take that to mean that those aliens come from somewhere beyond this world—that they don't live on this planet."

"So this simply adds to the puzzle," said Viona. "If they don't come from here, they must have come from some other planetary system because there seems to be no other world orbiting this sun."

"I'm afraid I have to agree," the Amazon acknowledged worriedly. "And from what we saw a little while ago, it doesn't appear that they're taking these people for slaves. There's something going on in this system and I can't figure out what it is."

Clicking on her wrist radio, she called Abna and updated him. "At the moment we're with some of the aboriginal natives. There seems to be a lot happening here. One of those alien spacecraft landed for a powwow with them using some kind of crystal thought-transfer instrument. Did you discover anything?"

"I'll say we did, Vi," came Abna's voice. "After a brush with an erupting volcano we came upon some kind of temple built into a cliff side. It's truly massive and clearly it hasn't been built by these primitives."

Moving the small switch, the Amazon replied, "I doubt if we can get much from the cave dwellers here. We're returning to the *Ultra*. I think we need to discuss this situation in detail before deciding what to do next."

CHAPTER IV

BACK on board the *Ultra*, it was the Amazon who spoke first, detailing how they had seen the alien spaceship land and how the cave dwellers had been summoned by those on board. It was when she again mentioned the curious device that the leader had used to communicate with the primitives that Abna showed intense interest.

"You say it looked like some kind of crystal and that somehow it remained on the native's forehead?"

"That's exactly what happened," the Amazon confirmed.

Pursing his lips, Abna searched through his immense knowledge of telepathic communication, seeking any memory of such a thing. Finally, he nodded. "I don't know of any inanimate crystal which could do that and since you say this device remained in place, my guess is that it was a living thing."

Perplexed, the others simply stared at him.

"I'm merely guessing here but it's quite feasible that some creatures communicate among themselves by telepathy. They extrude extremely fine sensory filaments directly into the subject's brain. It would pick up the alien's thoughts and transmit them straight into the recipient's mind."

"So this race is controlling these aboriginals in this way," Mexone said. "The question is—for what purpose? We saw no evidence they need them for workers."

Abna leaned forward over the table. "Unless it was to build that huge temple we found." He hesitated for a moment before going on. "I know it sound ridiculous to suggest a race only just slightly more evolved than the apes to be capable of such a feat—but it's the only suggestion I can make."

"It's certainly worth looking into," the Amazon acquiesced. "Somewhere there has to be a way to fit all these pieces of the puzzle together, if we can only find it."

Yawning, Viona said, "I suggest we all eat and then get some sleep. After that, we may be able to think more clearly. All that heat and humidity out there has been exhausting."

"I agree," the Amazon nodded emphatically. "It's already getting late. We'll make further plans in the morning—not that there are any mornings on this world."

While the others slept, the ever-active Amazon sat in the observation well, staring out at the eternal murk around the vessel. A host of unconnected thoughts were racing through her mind. She felt certain they were missing something—that there was a vital link between everything that had happened. And unless they discovered what it was they would not get much further in solving the puzzle presented by these aliens who seemingly appeared from nowhere and vanished in the same manner.

They knew that this race was stealing both the atmosphere and material from the outermost planet. But where were they taking this cargo? They were certainly not bringing it to this world. It already possessed an atmosphere—even if it was a thick, humid one.

An hour passed. Outside the ship, the nocturnal noises of the jungle echoed across the trees. Getting to her feet, she crossed to the window and peered out. In the gloom it was almost impossible to make out any detail. She could just see the dark shadow of the trees on the far edge of the clearing.

Occasionally, she noticed a black, monstrous shape moving among them but whatever they were they made no attack against the *Ultra*. Going back to the table, she sat down, attempting to put her chaotic thoughts into some kind of order. An instant later, she jerked up her head, everything else forgotten as she picked out the voice.

It was faint, almost inaudible, but by ignoring everything else, she managed to make out the words.

"Strangers from that far distant world... I have no way of knowing if my words can reach your minds—or where you are—but we desperately need your help. Xendor is even now under attack from that enemy. Powerful bombs are already raining down upon the surface. Soon I fear...."

Here, the voice faded completely. Tensely, the Amazon waited to see if it would resume its message—but there was nothing.

Rising swiftly, she ran across to the bunk where Abna lay sleeping and shook him urgently by the shoulder.

He woke at once, instantly alert. "What is it, Vi?"

"Those people we met on that other planet. I picked up one of their voices in my mind a few moments ago. They are being attacked and asking for our aid."

Swinging his legs to the floor, Abna stood up. "What exactly did the voice say, Vi?"

"That powerful bombs are raining down on the surface. If we don't stop them, they'll break through that outer surface and ravage everything inside. An entire people stand to be wiped out by these aggressors."

"Wake the others. I'll start the engines. But even at top speed, it will take some time to reach them." Without waiting for a reply, he ran to the controls and flung himself down in the chair.

By the time the other Crusaders were awake, and racing to their positions, the engines had built up to a thunderous roar. Smoothly, the *Ultra* lifted off from the surface, streaking through the dense atmosphere as they velocity increased steadily.

The Amazon came to sit beside him, peering through the visiscreen as they broke clear of the atmosphere and entered outer space. Ahead of them, the multitudinous stars of the Milky Way glittered in a broad band across the heavens.

Swiftly, the Amazon computed the course for Xendor as behind them, the curiously pulsing sun grew appreciably smaller.

"I only hope we're in time to save them," she said grimly. "The thought of a peaceful race such as the Xendorians being destroyed by aggressors such as these appalls me."

"Well, they'll have us to deal with now," Viona declared, standing before the screen, her hands on her hips.

"We're making the best speed we can taking into consideration we'll have to decelerate while we're some distance from the planet," Abna said. "My estimate is that we should reach Xendor within two hours at this velocity."

In the telescopic view it was just possible to pick out the planet as a tiny dot against the thousands of stars. Slowly, it grew larger.

"We should be able to spot their ships quite easily," Mexone put in, "with no atmosphere to give them any cover."

Busy at the controls, Abna said, "You can check on that while I reduce our velocity."

Gradually, Xendor swelled to a faint white disc as the ice-covered surface came into view. So far, there had been no further mental communication from the Xendorians but less than five minutes later, the voice echoed once more in their minds. Now, it was stronger than before and the urgency in it was clearly detectable.

Strangers from the planet Earth—can you hear me? We are still under attack and I fear the outer shield will not hold much longer. Once it is pierced we will lose all of our atmosphere and then only death awaits us.

Still operating the controls, Abna replied, consciously mentally projecting his words: "We can hear you clearly. At the moment we are some ten thousand miles from Xendor. Just hold on. We will deal with these aliens."

There followed a brief pause, then: From our temperature recorders on the surface, we believe they are attacking on the spaceward side of our world. How many of their vessels there are, we do not know. But take great care, you are only one vessel and there may be several of them.

This time the Amazon replied, "Have no fear for us. We have encountered such aggressive people before and know how to deal with them."

The mental voice fell silent. A few moments later, Thania called, "I can see them!" She turned away from the telescopic screen. "Three of them quiet close to the surface."

She stepped back a pace, rubbing her eyes, as a vicious flare empted on the planet.

"They just dropped a bomb. I could see the flash as it exploded."

"Right!" The Amazon turned in her chair. "Everyone to battle stations. Now let us see how these creatures like a taste of their own medicine."

As the *Ultra* dived out of the star-strewn heavens, the Crusaders were all able to see the tight formation of spaceships hovering above the planet. A second flash marked where another nuclear bomb had fallen. It erupted on the surface below. The *Ultra* came in low over the surface, just skimming the top of a mountain range, so that it approached the enemy vessels from the rear.

"Everyone ready?" the Amazon called. There was a chorus of affirmative replies. "Then let them have it!"

Deftly Viona thumbed a stud and a super-x-hydrogen bomb sped towards the rear enemy vessel. The impact was visible as a faint flash but what followed thereafter was something quite different. The entire spaceship exploded in a vivid flash of atomic flame

The detonation lit up the entire ground below, allowing the Crusaders a clear view of the deep craters gouged out of the planetary surface.

Almost at once, the remaining two attackers broke off their bombing of the surface, climbing away steeply as their commanders fought off their initial shock and surprise. A second hydrogen bomb narrowly missed its target as the alien ships sped in different directions.

"It certainly didn't take them long to recover," Abna remarked grimly. "Now they'll probably try to hit us from both sides."

"Let them try," the Amazon replied through her clenched teeth. "The *Ultra* can out-gun and out-maneuver them. I designed her and I'm absolutely sure of that, just as I'm sure of all the people who make up her crew. Now just keep them in sight all the time."

Swinging the nose of the *Ultra*, Abna ignored the vessel on their left and concentrated on the other. The distance between them narrowed swiftly as he applied more power to the engines. There was a sudden flash from the side of the enemy vessel. It was succeeded a couple of seconds later by another.

"They've launched some kind of weapon at us," Thania cried.

"Is the protective shield up, Abna?" the Amazon asked.

"Up and running," he replied. "Naturally, we don't know what kind of weapons these aliens have but the shield should protect us from any serious damage."

Moments later, the twin blasts struck the *Ultra*. The vessel juddered slightly and then resumed its normal course, swerving away from the surface of Xendor and heading after the alien vessel.

"They're using space torpedoes with nuclear warheads," the Amazon said after a brief pause. "The shield is sufficiently strong to absorb those blasts but I wouldn't like it to take too many of them. Any idea what that third vessel is doing?"

"It's swinging onto a course to bring it up behind us," Viona called. "It's staying out of range of our weapons. Probably saw what happened to the first ship."

Brushing back a strand of her blonde hair, the Amazon said harshly, "My guess is they'll try a pincer movement. If we can lure them into doing that, attacking us from both sides, there's a chance we can destroy them without firing a single shot."

Mystified, the others stared at her.

"How do you intend doing that?" Mexone asked finally. "I don't see how it's possible."

"You'll see. Move over Abna and let me have control of the *Ultra*."

Without a word, Abna vacated his seat and folded his arms across his chest. He had no idea what the Amazon meant to do but since she had designed and built this mighty vessel, she knew more than any of them about its limitations.

Placing her hands lightly on the controls, she swiftly increased the velocity and turned the nose of the *Ultra* until they had caught up with the second vessel. Smoothly, she adjusted their speed until they were flying alongside the enemy vessel with some two hundred miles separating them.

"You want me to send a broadside against them, mother?" Viona had hurried towards the firing controls and now stood ready.

"No. I want you to remain there until you see the flashes of their weapons. Let me know the second you spot them and then grab the nearest piece of equipment and hang on. Mexone, you go to the other side. If I'm right, that remaining vessel will close with us, hoping they can hit us simultaneously from both directions. Let me know the second they fire more torpedoes."

By the time everyone was in their places they were flying almost exactly midway between the enemy spacecraft. The tension in the control room heightened swiftly as the minutes dragged by.

Then both Viona and Mexone called out in almost the same moment. "Torpedoes on the way."

"Good. Everyone hang on tightly." Swiftly, the Amazon thrust forward the lever feeding power to the engines. Strain stood etched on all of their faces as the *Ultra* leapt forward like a maddened beast. Grasping anything they could, they somehow remained upright against the tremendous burst of acceleration. The maneuver took both enemy commanders completely by surprise. By the time they realized their own torpedoes were hurtling towards them through the space where the *Ultra* had been a moment earlier, it was too late.

Glancing into the rearward viewing screen, Thania let out a sudden excited yell. "You did it, Amazon. They've both been hit!"

The Amazon turned the *Ultra* slowly so that they all had a clear view of the stricken enemy vessels. Great gouts of flame erupted where the atomic torpedoes had struck. One of the spaceships was falling swiftly towards the planet, evidently completely out of control. The other was limping away towards deep space, badly damaged but still with its engines functioning.

"Do we follow that one and finish it off?" Viona asked.

The Amazon considered that proposition for a moment; then shook her head. "No. We're going to land as closely as possible to that other one. There may be survivors and if there are, I want to talk to them if possible."

"Talk to these murderers?" Abna interrupted in surprise. "This isn't like you, Vi. I would have thought you'd want such creatures killed for what they've tried to do here."

"That's true. Believe me, if this race cannot be persuaded to adopt peaceful attitudes towards their neighbors, I'll wipe them out completely without any qualms. But if it's at all possible, I want two questions answered before we go any further. I want to know where they come from—and I'd like to get my hands on one of those thought-transfer crystals they use on the cave dwellers."

Abna shrugged. "All right, we'll follow that spaceship down."

Now that the maneuver that had crippled the two alien ships had been successfully completed, the Amazon got up and Abna took over the controls once more. They could just make out the shape of the descending vessel against the pale glow of the ice-covered surface.

Still out of control and with atomic fires burning along a large part of the hull, its doomed fall was ended as it crashed near the base of a long mountain range.

Decelerating, the *Ultra* finally landed within a quarter of a mile of the crash. Turning to Mexone and Viona, the Amazon said briskly, "Thania—you remain on board with Abna. Mexone and Viona, get into your suits and come with me and remember, once we get out there, we may also have those ice creatures to contend with."

Ten minutes later, the three Crusaders were standing on the surface beside the huge bulk of the *Ultra*. With the Amazon in the lead, they trudged towards the mountains where the fiery glow of the crashed spaceship stood out like a blazing beacon against the eternal night.

For the moment, the thick layer of the frozen atmosphere seemed empty without any sign of the creatures they had earlier encountered. Pushing herself vigorously forward, the Amazon approached the crash site, her keen gaze taking in the details of the enemy vessel. It had evidently burst open on impact, splitting into a number of large segments.

The central portion was relatively intact, but it was clear that with the nuclear fires still raging inside, it would be highly dangerous to approach too close. Already, the small Geiger detectors they carried were registering a high level of radiation.

Pausing while still some distance away, the Amazon lifted a hand and pointed to their left. A large chunk of debris had been flung from the main section by the impact. Keeping their weapons in readiness, they walked towards it.

Several badly mangled bodies lay strewn on the ice around the twisted bulk of metal. A quick, cursory glance told them that all of these aliens were dead. Over the space radio, Viona said, "Somehow, I doubt if we'll find any alive. If the crash didn't kill them, that hard radiation and the explosions from those torpedoes would have."

"I just need one," the Amazon answered harshly. "Keep looking."

Reaching the large ragged hole in the side of the spaceship segment, the Amazon hauled herself inside, switching on the small, but powerful, torch she carried. Swiftly, the swung the brilliant beam around the interior. It was impossible to guess which part of the enemy vessel this was but the sides were lined with long instrument panels. Most of them were smashed and bent beyond repair.

A moment later, Viona joined her, leaving Mexone outside to keep watch for any sign of survivors—or the ice creatures.

There were two more bodies inside, their four arms and legs twisted unnaturally beneath them. The Amazon bent and turned them over, staring down into the hard, cruel features. Eyes without any pupil glared back at her in the torchlight.

"Ugly looking creatures, aren't they?" Viona said, repressing a shudder.

"Possibly we would appear ugly to them," her mother answered shortly. "There must be millions of different races scattered throughout the galaxy, all different from ourselves. It's well to remember that even the ugliest of them, according to our standards, may be the most peaceful and intelligent."

She turned her attention to the instruments but most of these were so alien in their appearance that she could make little of them. Then a sudden call from Mexone caused her to jerk up her head and move swiftly towards the opening.

Carefully avoiding the jagged edges of metal, she and Viona dropped lightly to the ground.

Mexone pointed towards the main section of the spaceship. Four figures had dropped from it onto the ice. Picking themselves up, they made to run, then stopped as they spotted the Crusaders. Swiftly, they flung themselves down onto the ice, drawing their weapons.

The Amazon flung herself sideways as a heat beam sizzled through the air where she had been standing. Jerking up her blaster she sent two rapid shows at the figures. One of them twisted violently and flopped onto the ice. The remaining three dropped out of sight into a small hollow.

More pencil-thin beams spat through the darkness, hitting the wreckage above the heads of the Crusaders as they flung themselves down. Sparks rained down all around them as they lay flat on the ice.

"It seems we have a stand-off," the Amazon muttered softly. Keeping her head well down, she glanced around them, then pointed. "Do you think you can work your way around them, Mexone?"

Giving a slight nod, Mexone slid away to his right, keeping his body pressed hard against the ground. Over the radio, the Amazon hissed, "Remember, I want at least one of them alive."

"I understand, Amazon," came the answer a moment later.

Turning to Viona, the Amazon said, "We'll give him some covering fire from here."

Without replying, the girl sent several shots over the ice to where the aliens lay hidden. Several times, not knowing the meaning of fear, she lifted her head to get a better shot into the distant low hollow.

Without looking round, she said quietly, "Do you think they'll try to make a run for it, mother?"

Shaking her head, the Amazon replied, "That isn't likely. With their spaceship completely wrecked there's nowhere for them to run. They'll stay here and fight it out to the end."

"I don't see any sign of Mexone. He should be in a position to see them by now."

"He'll open fire when he's ready." Despite her calmness, the Amazon was getting impatient. She was not used to being pinned down like this. For a moment, she considered getting to her feet and running forward, hoping to take the enemy by surprise—then realized the stupidity of such a rash act.

This race they were fighting were born killers who had no respect at all for any other form of life. They would commit any atrocity just so long as it served their purpose. With an effort, she forced the sudden surge of anger from her mind.

The next moment there came the flash of brilliance from a protonic blaster. Mexone had reached a place just a little way behind and to one side of the enemy. The Amazon saw one of the four-armed beings sudden rise up, teeter for an instant and then fall forward onto the ice.

The remaining two attackers mistakenly believed he was now the main danger and turned their fire on him. This gave the Amazon the chance she needed. Within seconds she was on her feet and racing forward as swiftly as possible over the treacherous surface with Viona only a short distance behind her.

Seeing her, Mexone stopped firing. The two aliens tried to turn to meet the danger. One died as the beam of protonic energy struck him in the middle of the chest, hurling him several feet across the ground. The second tried to bring his weapon to bear on the Amazon.

Before he could do so, she had leapt forward. One swift foot kicked the gun from his hand and the other landed hard on his body, pinning him to the ground. Swinging her clenched fist she hit him hard where his suit joined the base of the helmet. The alien slumped forward and lay still.

Straightening up, the Amazon said tersely. "I reckon that even I would have a little trouble pinning those four arms. Now we'll get him into the *Ultra*."

Hauling the unconscious alien upright, she bent and took his weight over one shoulder. This time they made it safely to the airlock without any interference from the marauding ice creatures. The Amazon carried him up the ladder and into the airlock. Once they were inside, she took him through to the control room where Abna stood waiting.

"I saw most of what was happening out there," he said as the Amazon lowered the ungainly body to the floor.

"We killed three of them," Viona told him, shrugging out of her suit. "None of the others on board appear to have survived the explosions and the crash."

Abna bent and turned the alien over, staring down into the cadaverous features. Then he glanced up. "Will it be safe to remove this suit?"

The Amazon nodded. "Those others we saw giving orders to the cave dwellers were obviously able to breathe the atmosphere there without protective helmets. He should be able to tolerate the air in here."

"Can you get into his mind so that we can communicate with him once he regains consciousness?" Viona queried.

"I've had quite a bit of success with aliens in the past," Abna replied, smiling. "Unless these creatures are capable of putting up a mental block to shield their thoughts, I think I can do it."

Ever impatient to be doing something, the Amazon asked, "Is there no way we can bring him round?"

"I doubt it." Abna examined the alien more closely. "You certainly hit him hard enough, Vi. I'm surprised he isn't dead with a broken neck. However, I would suggest we chain him up before he does recover. With those four arms, he could do quite a bit of damage before we could fully restrain him."

Biting her lip, the Amazon said, "Sorry. That hadn't occurred to me. We'll chain him down securely on one of the acceleration couches."

Once the alien's protective suit had been removed and he had been securely shackled, Abna returned to the controls. "I'd better take the *Ultra* into space just in case those ice things are around. We had enough trouble with them the last time."

"Good thinking," Mexone said.

Starting the engines, Abna lifted the *Ultra* from the surface, putting the vessel into automatic control around the planet before returning to where their prisoner lay on the couch. After a short while, the alien stirred. His eyes flicked open. Then he seemed to recognize what had happened. Muscles strained beneath his tunic but the metal chains were far too strong to be broken. Finally, recognizing the futility of attempting to free himself, he lay back and glared at his captors.

Bending, Abna placed his large hand on the alien's forehead. The man tried to jerk his head away but Abna merely clamped his grip more firmly. No one in the room spoke or made any movement as Abna concentrating on absorbing the other's language from his mind. Minutes passed and then Abna straightened up.

"Did you succeed?" the Amazon asked tensely.

Abna nodded slowly. Lines of strain showed clearly on his broad forehead. "It wasn't easy," he admitted. "In fact, it was far more difficult than I imagined. Not only was there a mental block as I'd feared but his mental capabilities are really exceptional. Not quite in the super-mind league—such as the Mizanu we encountered near Alpha Centauri for instance—but powerful enough. He almost managed to control my mind."

"Which explains why Idron's people were unable to read their minds," the Amazon said. "But at least you can communicate with him?"

"Yes—I can do that. Whether he will tell us anything is another matter."

"See if you can get him to tell us where they come from," the Amazon went on. "Clearly it isn't here or on that other planet. If it's from some other solar system we'll make him point it out to us on the star map of this region."

Viona glanced at her in mild surprise. "Surely you don't intend to take on an entire solar system?"

"We'll consider the options once we get the truth out of him," the Amzon retorted thinly. "Begin questioning him, Abna, and make him understand that we're deadly serious and want the truth; that we're not to be trifled with."

Standing over the alien, all seven foot of blond giant, Abna spoke several words in a harsh, guttural tone.

Thinning his lips, their captive hissed a long string of syllables, then turned his head to one side as if indicating he intended to say nothing more.

"Well?" the Amazon demanded. "What did you ask him?"

"I asked him where he and his kind come from. He said… He said he has no wish to speak to inferiors and that if we do not release him, the rest of the fleet will come and annihilate us."

An expression of intense anger flashed across the Amazon's beautiful features. For a moment, she seemed on the point of lashing out with her fist. Then she controlled herself with an effort. Grasping one of the alien's hands in a grip of steel-like strength, she said icily, "I don't believe in torture but in this case I might make an exception. Tell him that if he doesn't answer our questions, I'll break every bone in his body."

Slowly, she twisted the man's wrist until he uttered a sudden yelp of agony.

Abna repeated his question. The alien remained silent, only his eyes moving as he glared first at one of the Crusaders and then at the others.

Slowly, the Amazon increased the pressure, forcing his hand back. A second scream of pain was followed by a sudden torrent of words.

"He says he's willing to talk," Abna translated. "According to him, his race comes from a planet he calls Abilon."

"Ask him where that planet is situated. Tell him we'll show him star maps so that he can point it out to us."

Abna put the question and listened intently to the other's reply. His brows were drawn down in an expression of puzzlement as he faced the Amazon. "From what I can make out, Abilon is not in some other star system, it's here in this one."

"That's impossible," the Amazon declared emphatically. "Either he's deliberately lying to throw us off the track—or there is a third planet in this system which we've somehow overlooked."

"That might just be the case," Abna mused. "If you remember, Vi, some of the early astronomers on Earth believed there was a planet lying between Mercury and the Sun. They even gave it a name—Vulcan."

"Yes, but later observations showed it was just a mistake, almost certainly nothing more than a perfectly round sunspot moving across Sol's surface."

"That's right," Abna agreed. "But it may be there is one in this case. It's something we must look into before we dismiss what he's said. After all, when we first sighted those spaceships they were moving sunward, not into outer space heading for some other system."

The Amazon nodded reluctantly. "Very well. I doubt if we'll get anything more of importance from him." She glanced down at the tunic the alien was wearing, then went on, "From that insignia he has on his chest I'd say he's some kind of leader, just like the one we saw talking with the cave men. If he is, it's just possible that—"

Without releasing her hold on the captive's wrist, she reached down with her free hand and slipped it inside the pocket. At this movement, the prisoner twisted violently, struggling to free himself.

"What is it you're looking for?" Thania asked.

The Amazon withdrew her hand, holding something in her clenched fingers. "This," she said, holding it out in the light so they could all see it. "I thought there might be a chance he would be carrying one with him."

The object was a small oval crystal which flashed with a myriad colors where the light caught it.

Viona gave a gasp of surprise and recognition. "It's one of those thought-transfer crystals they used on those aboriginals."

"Precisely. With this we can communicate with the cave dwellers."

"To what end, Amazon?" Mexone asked.

"I'm interested in what is inside that temple Abna and Thania discovered on that planet. I doubt if we'll get the truth from him." She inclined her head towards the shackled alien. "But those cave dwellers may be able to tell us. I'm more convinced than ever that there is something inside that temple which is the key to this whole mystery."

"Then if you're right," Thania interrupted, "all we have to do is get that information from those primitives and somehow find a way into that place we found."

Glancing down at their captive, Abna said in a serious tone, "What do we do with him?"

The Amazon shrugged almost negligently. "What we mean to do with the rest of his race when we catch up with them. Kill him. He's no longer of any use to us."

Abna studied her closely as she made to turn away, "I know how you feel about this race, Vi. But we can't simply kill a prisoner in cold blood. That would be nothing short of murder."

"Then what do you think we should do? Give him the run of the ship, never knowing when he'll kill us? Why should he be any different from all those others we've killed during our journeying through the galaxy? Our task is to root out evil and oppression wherever we find it—and destroy those who practice it."

"Yes, but all of those others were armed and it was either them or us."

"May I make a suggestion?" Viona butted in. "Why not lock him securely in one of the spare cabins? Keep him chained and then turn him over to those cave men once we reach their planet? I'm sure they'll know what to do with him."

There was an undisguised reluctance in the Amazon's voice as she answered, "All right, But at the first sign of any trouble from him—he dies. Is that understood?"

Hauling the alien upright, Abna caught one of his arms in an unbreakable grip and thrust him out of the control room. He came back a few minutes later. "He's safely secure," he said in answer to the Amazon's look of mute inquiry. "I think he recognizes the futility of trying to get away."

"Good. Now we have to decide on our next step."

"Somehow, I think you've already decided," Viona said. "We're going back to the other planet to find out what lies within that temple. With that thing you took from the alien, you should be able to get some information from those cave people."

"That's exactly what I have in mind." The Amazon turned to glance at the others. "Unless any of you have a better idea."

For a moment there was silence. Then Mexone said, "Perhaps we should get in touch with those people inside this world—let them know what has happened and that they're safe from attack—at least for the present."

The Amazon gave an acquiescent nod. She consciously put her words into thoughts: "If you can hear me, Idron, your world is safe for the time being. Two of the enemy's vessels have been destroyed and the third has limped off into space."

There was a momentary pause and then Idron's mental voice came into all of their minds.

We are all indeed grateful for what you have done for us, people of Earth. It is indeed fortunate for us that you came. What are your plans now?

This time it was Abna who replied. "We are returning to that other world in your solar system. There is something there that we believe may enable us to determine why your sun is behaving in such a peculiar manner. Since there is nothing on your world that may account for it, this would seem to be the logical place to look."

Then we hope you are successful in your search. Perhaps you will return soon so that we may know what has happened. For a few moments, the mental voice echoed in their minds—then there was silence.

Once Abna had plotted in the course for the jungle planet, the Crusaders relaxed with the exception of the Amazon who moved restlessly from one observation window to the next keeping a watchful eye for the damaged enemy vessel.

Although she made a diligent search of the entire heavens, there was no sign of it.

CHAPTER V

THE journey back to the inner planet was uneventful. There was still no sign of the crippled enemy vessel. Either the atomic fires on board when it had been hit by their companion vessel had consumed it entirely—or those on board had managed to extinguish the flames and limp homeward—back to wherever that was.

As they approached the planet, Abna consulted the radar map they had made of the surface the last time they had visited this cloud-enshrouded world. Despite the fact that no details were visible from space, the chart was accurate in every detail. Viona and Thania came to stand beside him.

"This is that volcano we almost crashed into, Thania," he said, jabbing his finger at the map.

Turning, he motioned to the Amazon to join them. "Plotting back along the course we took, our landing place would be here. Since you traveled west from this point, Vi, I would say the cave dwellers live here. Now—which do we visit first?"

"The cave people," the Amazon said without any hesitation.

"Any particular reason for that choice?"

"Two reasons," replied the Amazon crisply. "First, I want to show them our captive. That should be sufficient to let them know these people are not gods as these aboriginals imagine, but just ordinary beings. Secondly, I intend to use this—" she took out the strange crystal and held it out in the palm of her hand. "If it is possible to communicate with them, I mean to ask them about this temple and what might be inside it."

"That seems logical," Abna admitted. "Then we put the *Ultra* down right outside those caves."

Twenty minutes later, the *Ultra* descended through the cloud layer and landed in almost exactly the same space as the alien vessel had done. Switching off the engines, Abna joined the others at the airlock.

The Amazon had dragged their captive from the small room where he had been kept locked up. There was a sullen expression on the alien's thin features as he struggled ineffectually against the chains binding his arms.

Viona threw him a swift glance. "How is he going to make his way down the ladder with his arms bound?" she asked. "We daren't take those chains off."

"I'll get him down," her mother replied grimly. "Since these people regard me as some kind of chief, I should demonstrate I'm the one they can look up to."

As the airlock slid open, she grabbed the alien by the legs and hoisted him across one shoulder, signaling the others to go down.

There was no sign of the cave people as they slowly descended the ladder. At the bottom, the Amazon said, "They may think we are that other race and are waiting for that call the alien made. Once we show ourselves, however, I'm quite sure they'll recognize me. When we were last here, they looked on me as the leader of their tribe."

Stepping forward, she gave three loud whistles. For a moment, there was no sign of any activity. Then the aboriginals emerged in small groups, staring up at the mighty bulk of the spaceship as if recognizing it was not the one that had come before, then peering mutely at the Crusaders.

Among them, the Amazon was surprised to see the huge figure of the aboriginal she had bested in the contest of strength. For a moment, the other stared at her. Then his glance slid away and he looked down at the ground at his feet.

"Isn't he the one who—?" Viona began.

The Amazon nodded. "Evidently, he returned once we left. Once we were gone, he must have reinstated himself as leader. Somehow, I don't think we'll have any trouble from him. He knows which of us is the stronger. My guess is he'll be only too willing to co-operate. I doubt if he wants to be shown up in front of the others again."

Walking up to him, the Amazon tossed the bound alien onto the ground at the aboriginal's feet where he lay groaning at the bone-shaking impact.

Taking the strange crystal from her belt, the Amazon held it out for a moment so that the gigantic cave man could see it. From the flash of expression in his deep-set eyes, she knew he had instantly recognized it.

Reaching forward, she placed it on the other's forehead. As before, it remained there when she took her hand away. Clearly, Abna's suggestion that it was a living thing was close to the truth.

Focusing her thoughts on the crystal, she pointed towards the alien lying on the ground close by and then formed a picture of the alien spacecraft in her mind. Then she deliberately emptied her own mind of all other thoughts, hoping to receive some mental reply back in return. But there was nothing. It was as if the other's thought processes were incapable of projecting mental images.

Sighing in exasperation, she turned to Abna. "There's nothing. I tried to form a picture in his mind of the alien spacecraft hoping I might get some information as to why these aliens come here."

"Let me try. It's possible those aliens have been coming here on a regular basis for years. Maybe he doesn't associate it with anything of particular importance."

"So, what do you mean to do?" The Amazon sounded piqued by the fact that she had failed to get any information.

"I'm going to project an image of that temple, or whatever it is, into his mind. He may know nothing about it, of course. Probably these people don't wander too far from their caves. But it may be that he's seen it for himself."

Stepping up to the cave dweller, Abna shaped his thoughts and focused them on the crystal still clinging limpet-wise on the man's forehead. Mentally, he pictured the massive building as he had seen it, carved from the solid rock of the cliff with the huge metal doors set in the center.

This time there was a response from the other. A look of wonder and awe passed over the brutish features and he put one hand up to his forehead. Abna kept the image focused in his mind, concentrating all of his mental efforts on it, hoping to impress it clearly on the aboriginal's mind. But suddenly, without any effort on his part, it changed.

It was the same place but seen from a different angle. Clearly, the cave man was projecting an image of his own, a vivid memory which had clearly remained in his subconscious. There was one of the enemy spaceships in the background and a number of the aliens standing in front of the gates.

One of the aliens lifted a hand and pointed it at the great doors, clearly saying something at the same time. Slowly, the doors opened inward. Abna had immediately grasped that somehow that powerful memory of the creature in front of him was being projected into his mind through the action of the crystal acting as a strange intermediary.

Clearly, the other had been there at that time, standing somewhere to the side of the smooth plateau. Accordingly, it was difficult to see what lay beyond the doors. There was light of some kind inside, illuminating several large cables running across the smooth floor and he had the impression of a large pedestal with something resting on it.

From the acute angle he was viewing it he could ascertain nothing about the nature of this object. It was clearly connected to the cables he saw and absorbing power from them. The one who had opened the doors motioned to the other aliens standing near the base of the spaceship.

Three of them stepped forward and followed him inside the chamber, passing out of sight. After several minutes, they reappeared. Turning, the leader said something and the massive doors swung shut once more.

A moment later, the image faded.

With a thoughtful expression on his handsome features, Abna gently removed the thought-transference device from the cave man's forehead and handed it to the Amazon.

"Well?" she asked, a trifle impatiently. "Did you learn anything?"

"Actually, I learned quite a lot from him—but not quite as much as I would've liked. It seems he's been to that temple before. How many times, I don't know—but he went there with these aliens. He has an extremely vivid memory in his mind and, somehow, with that crystal, he was able to project that recollection into my mind."

As he hesitated, Thania butted in, a touch of excitement in her voice. "Did that image show you how we might get inside that place, Abna? When we saw it, those huge doors looked impenetrable."

"From what I saw, one of the aliens pointed at the doors, said something, and then they opened."

"Rather like 'Open Sesame'," the Amazon said musingly.

Thania stared blankly at her, the words meaning nothing to her.

Smiling a little, the Amazon went on, "It's something from a very old story often told on Earth—secret doors that can only be opened by saying the magic words."

"Then that doesn't help us," Mexone argued. "We don't know the magic words, unless—" He threw a meaningful glance at the alien lying on the ground a few feet away. "Unless we can make him tell us."

Abna considered that possibility for a moment and then shook his head. "If this thing—whatever it is—is concealed in such a fashion, it must be extremely important to this race. My guess is that only one, perhaps two, of them has that information. It's unlikely he's one of them."

"There's no harm in trying," the Amazon said with a trace of iron in her voice. "I mean to get to the bottom of this mystery by whatever means necessary. A little arm-twisting will make him talk."

Bending, she grasped the front of the alien's tunic and pulled him easily upright, holding him still as he struggled to free himself. Without taking her eyes off him, she said, "Ask him if he knows how to open the doors of that building, Abna. I'll know if he's telling the truth."

Shrugging, Abna uttered a string of words; words that were unintelligible to the others. On hearing them, the alien jerked up his head and a startled expression flashed across his angular features.

"Obviously, he's surprised that we know anything about that place," the Amazon said thinly as she waited for the alien's reply.

For a moment it seemed the other did not intend to answer, his thin lips pressed tightly together. Tightening her grip, the Amazon raised her arm slightly, and lifted him off the ground, his legs dangling helplessly.

"Tell him he either answers us truthfully, or I'll throw him off the edge of this plateau onto the rocks at the bottom." Turning, she began walking towards the precipitous drop a hundred yards away.

Abna said something more to the alien, but it seemed the man had already guessed the Amazon's intention from the tone of her voice. He was also aware of her ability to do exactly as she said.

Swiftly, he let out a long string of gutturals. "What did he say?" Still holding the captive off the ground, the Amazon paused.

"He said the only thing inside that so-called temple is an instrument they purposely left on the planet so that these creatures would regard it as a god and the place would be considered sacred to them. That way they would ensure no other tribes might go anywhere in its vicinity. The only thing in there is a useless piece of metal."

"And he expects us to believe that?"

"Don't you?" Mexone queried.

The Amazon shook her blonde head. "Not a word of it. He may fool these pathetic creatures but not me. He's lying."

"How can you be so sure of that?" Thania asked. "He must be sufficiently intelligent to know he can expect no help from his friends. As far as they're concerned, he died in the crash on that planet so what has he got to lose by telling us the truth?"

"Quite a lot I think. If that image you got from this aboriginal is exactly what happened to him—why would a useless piece of metal require power cables fitted to it? No. From what you saw in that cave dweller's mind, Abna, something in that place is absorbing one heck of a lot of energy, possibly from some nuclear generator they have inside."

"That makes sense, I suppose," Abna admitted.

"Then tell him what I think and ask him again if he knows how to open those doors. If he still refuses to co-operate, I'll carry out my threat. And just to convince him I mean every word—"

Breaking off in mid-sentence, the Amazon carried the alien to the very edge of the steep drop. Extending her arm, she held him out over the rim.

A look of terror creased the man's features as he glanced down into the abyss that lay beneath his dangling feet. The muscles in his arms bulged as he tried desperately to break the chains. Then he sagged visibly.

His voice was little more than a terrified croak as he spoke rapidly, almost too quickly for Abna to pick out the words.

Abna translated. "He says he can open those doors but there is nothing there which can be of any interest to us."

"We'll make up our own minds about that once we find out what it is." The Amazon held the captive there for another minute, then drew back and lowered him to the ground where he stood swaying helplessly. "Get him back into the *Ultra*," she said, giving the alien a violent shove in the back that sent him spinning to the ground.

"I presume we're going to that so-called temple," Abna said, grabbing the fallen man and dragging him towards the spacecraft.

"We are," the Amazon replied decisively. "And I'm hoping to find some answers to this puzzle there. At the moment, things don't seem to be making too much sense. There are still a lot of questions which must be answered before we have the full picture of what's going on here."

"I hope you find what you want but we must remember that we're dealing with an alien science here. It's unlikely that this race developed a scientific technology that matches our own. Even if we find something there, we may not be able to understand it."

The Amazon let that pass. Following the others into the airlock, she closed the heavy door and locked it. Abna set the bound alien in one of the chairs and motioned to Mexone to keep an eye on him. At the moment, however, all of the fight seemed to have gone out of him. For the first time, it seemed, his race had come up against one not only equally intelligent but physically much stronger.

Once the *Ultra* was in the air, Abna set a course eastward while the others stood at the observation windows, keeping a close look out for the volcano that lay directly in their path. The Amazon's keen eyes caught the ominous red glow of the eruption while it was still only a faint pinkish smudge on the clouds, enabling Abna to alter their course well in time to avoid it.

Very soon, they came within sight of the wide river winding its sluggish way across the landscape and there, directly ahead of them, stood the high escarpment. It utterly dwarfed the land around it, the dark-green area of swamp to their left and the few scattered regions of low, stunted bushes.

Standing beside Abna, the Amazon eyed it with an all-embracing, speculative glance. It sheer massiveness made it stand out from everything else in the vicinity. It completely dominated the distant skyline.

Finally, Viona remarked, "It's easy to see why these aliens chose this one spot on the planet to conceal something important. On this primeval jungle world I doubt if there's anything else like it."

"Perhaps," the Amazon said dryly, "but mere natural formations are of no real interest to me. The Grand Canyon on Earth is something similar to this. I'm only interested in what is concealed inside it."

Descending slowly on its atomic exhaust, the *Ultra* landed with scarcely a bump under Abna's expert hands. The airlock was opened and with Abna manhandling their prisoner, they descended the ladder and approached the mighty doors in the cliff side, flanked by their equally gigantic stone pillars.

Eyeing the scene, the Amazon remarked, "I fully agree that this could only have been built by these aliens. Even if they acted under their orders, the primitives could never have produced anything on this magnificent scale."

Their captive was thrust forward, his hands still bound. Turning to Abna, the alien said something.

"What did he say?" the Amazon asked.

"He says the ritual for opening these doors is very precise. He has to have one hand free."

"Very well. Loosen one of the chains. If he tries to escape, he won't get far out here in the open."

Very carefully, Abna unlocked the chain binding the alien's right upper arm. In the background, both Viona and Mexone stood with their hands close to their weapons, ready for any sign of trickery.

Slowly, the alien lifted his arm until his finger was pointing directly at the doors. Harsh gutturals, interspersed with liquid piping syllables came from his lips.

The Crusaders watched expectantly. For a few moments, nothing happened. Then soundlessly, the doors swung inward on cleverly concealed hinges.

Turning to Mexone, the Amazon said tautly, "You stay here, Mexone, and make sure he doesn't try to remove those other chains."

She commenced to walk towards the gaping orifice in the rock; then paused. "On second thoughts, bring him with us."

Abna glanced at her. "If this thing is something so alien that it's beyond even our comprehension, Vi, I doubt if he could explain it to us, even if we forced him to talk."

The Amazon's full lips twisted into a grim smile. "I wasn't thinking about that. It just occurred to me that if we left him outside, he could speak the words to close those doors and we would all be trapped inside. Judging by the thickness of these doors, I doubt if we would ever get out."

"You're right, Amazon," Mexone spoke as he jabbed the alien in the back with the barrel of his blaster, prodding him forward. "That's probably what he had in mind when he told us he could open them."

In a loose bunch they stepped inside the interior of the cliff. All around them, a pale greenish radiance gave them plenty of illumination by which to see every detail although none of them could see where the light came from. It seemed to permeate the air from every conceivable direction. The huge metal pedestal that Abna had described earlier stood in the exact center of the chamber.

From the middle of the three walls, large cables snaked across the smooth floor, each terminating in a junction from which five smaller leads were linked into the back of the most peculiar machine they had ever seen. Indeed, it was not very easy to see it at all since it was surrounded by a twisting, diaphanous haze that seemed to be spinning in all directions at once.

Momentarily Thania turned away, putting her hand over her eyes. "What can it be?" she gasped. "Whatever it is, it hurts my eyes just to look at it."

With a supreme effort, the Amazon forced her twisting vision to right itself. Within the oddly gyrating haze, she made out something composed of angles that were acute and obtuse at the same time. There were edges that appeared to stretch away into infinity and it was spinning so rapidly that it blurred in and out of sight in a manner that caused her stomach muscles to churn nauseously.

Moistening her lips, she said hoarsely, "I wouldn't advise anyone to look at it for too long. That hazy kind of shield may be some kind of plasma but normally that form of matter must be kept within some special sort of vessel. I must confess I've never seen anything like this before."

"Nor have I," Abna admitted. "Obviously, by the look of all those cables, it's atomic-powered. I would say there are three nuclear power plants here, one behind each of those walls, supplying it with an endless, and powerful, source of energy. I would suggest that everyone keeps well away from it until we can get some idea of what it is."

"And how do we do that?" Viona asked. "Here we are, the best scientific brains in the Solar System, yet this thing has beaten us."

"Only because it's been made by an alien science," the Amazon said in a slightly admonishing tone. "While it's possible this race has advanced well in excess of us, it is more likely their scientific evolution has taken a different path to ours. We know they have nuclear energy. Their spacecraft appear to be driven by it and those were nuclear warheads they were using."

While she had been speaking, Abna had moved forward a little way despite his warning to the others. He was peering into at the alien machine, his brow creased in concentration, his eyes narrowed to mere slits.

Then he said, "If you want my opinion, this is something that has been argued about in scientific circles for more than a century but everyone considered it impossible. Do you know what that thing is in the center, spinning so fast that it must be approaching the speed of light along its edges?"

When the others shook their head in bewilderment, he went on, "I'm sure it's a tesseract."

"A what—?" Mexone asked.

Nodding slightly, the Amazon explained. "A tesseract is the name given to a hypothetical four-dimensional cube. It's a purely mathematical term. A dot has zero dimensions, a line is one-dimensional, a square has two dimensions, and a cube has three."

"And a tesseract is the next step up in the mathematical series," Abna said.

"Unfortunately, with our three-dimensional minds, we can't visualize a tesseract," the Amazon went on. "It's only a mathematical concept—until now. Somehow, these aliens have constructed one and I would say that it is spinning inside an extremely intense magnetic— or electrical—field."

"But to what purpose?" Thania had little knowledge of what the Amazon was describing.

Shrugging, Abna said, "I suppose your guess is as good as mine, Thania. It's obvious this instrument is producing some kind of force but its exact nature is beyond even me, unless—"

He broke off abruptly, stood a short distance from the pedestal and peered up at the smooth dome over their heads. Scanning the curved surface minutely, he suddenly uttered an exclamation. "I was right. Look up there, almost at the top of that wall." He pointed.

The others followed the direction he was indicating. There was a small hole that had evidently been drilled all the way through the enclosing rock to the outside. Glancing back at the machine on the pedestal, he said excitedly, "This instrument is projecting an extremely narrow beam of some kind of energy through that hole and my guess is that it's aimed directly at the sun."

"At the sun?" Mexone uttered the exclamation of surprise.

"Yes. You remember when we first approached this planet, we reckoned it always turns one hemisphere towards the sun. This force beam is aligned exactly on it—and I think I know why."

The same thought occurred to the Amazon. "I think you're right, Abna. This instrument is some highly sophisticated form of time-distorter. Once it approaches that sun the beam somehow expands tremendously and encloses the luminary within a huge time-warp."

"And that explains why this sun is pulsating so rapidly. As Viona put it—like a beating heart in the middle of the galaxy. Inside that time-sphere, time is speeded up tremendously. We know there are thousands, possibly millions of stars in the galaxy that, during their evolution, pass through a period of instability when they pulsate. This lasts for a few million years and then they settle down to a more normal existence."

"So that's what would normally happen with this sun," Thania said, "but this thing here has speeded up that process."

"If Abna is right, that seems to be the case," the Amazon explained. "Instead of pulsating once in months or a few years, this is happening every two or three minutes."

Abna bent and peered closely at the tiered banks of controls situated near the base of the pedestal, then straightened up, shaking his head. "I can't make any sense of them. Perhaps if I—"

He broke off sharply. While they had all been concentrating on the machine, they had temporarily taken their eyes off the alien. During their conversation, he had backed slowly away from them. Now he turned and began to run for the opening. Despite being partially shackled, his long legs carried him swiftly as he darted from side to side.

Almost without thinking, the Amazon leapt after him, knowing that once he gained the outside, he had only to speak those words to shut the great doors on them. By the time she reached the entrance, the alien was still several yards ahead of her. Inside the chamber, the others were unable to use their weapons for fear of hitting her.

The alien suddenly skidded to a halt, whirled, and pointed his free hand at the doors. In the same instant, the Amazon acted.

Twisting, she leapt through the air straight for him. Before he could open his mouth, she swung her arm in a swift arc. The side of her hand slammed against his neck.

Without uttering a single cry, he fell back onto the hard ground with the Amazon on top of him. She instantly tensed her arm to deliver another blow—but it was unnecessary. The man's head lay limply on one side. His neck was broken.

Getting to her feet, she gave him only a cursory glance and then walked back to the others. "He won't give us any more trouble," she said grimly. "I suppose we should have anticipated he might try to do something like that."

"It was my fault entirely," Mexone said. "I was supposed to be keeping an eye on him."

"There's no harm done." The Amazon turned her attention back to the time machine, studying it intently. "The question now is— what are we going to do now we know what's happening?"

"If there is any way we can destroy this—or at least put it out of action—that would be the best course," Viona suggested. "At least, it should bring that sun out there back onto a more normal course of evolution."

"That's true," the Amazon agreed. "But in this case I doubt if the best course is the wisest one."

"You don't mean to destroy it?" Thania looked surprised. "Surely we could plant some nuclear device with a timing mechanism and be well away before this entire chamber is blown apart."

"Of course, we could. But when you begin to tinker with time, it can have unexpected, and sometimes disastrous, consequence. I'd prefer to know a little more about this sun and where this alien race fit into the puzzle before I do anything so drastic."

"So we leave this place wide open?" Thania gave a brief shrug. "And if any of these aboriginals should stumble on it?"

"That isn't likely. Even if they do, I'm convinced they would never dare to enter this place. They've all been brainwashed into believing this is a place of their god. That would be a good enough reason for them staying well away from it."

After giving the huge chamber a final glance to make sure she had not missed anything important, the Amazon turned and led the way outside. The dead alien lay where he had fallen. Giving the body only a brief glance, the Crusaders walked back to the *Ultra*.

Once they were settled comfortably in their seats, Abna started the engines and they lifted off, passing through the atmosphere within minutes. The sun, still performing its strange antics, lay almost directly ahead of them—and there was something else; something which brought the Amazon leaping from her seat. From that distance, it was only just visible as a faint, hazy patch but it set alarm bells ringing in the Amazon's head.

Swiftly, she crossed to the screen and connected the ultra-telescope to the viewer, adjusting the fine controls until the image was brilliantly sharp. Her sudden intake of breath brought Viona and Thania immediately to her side.

"What can that be?" Thania queried, frowning.

"Spaceships," the Amazon replied, "and from what I can see, there must be at least a hundred of them. My guess is that that crippled vessel managed to limp home and give the alarm. Now the entire alien fleet it out hunting for us!"

CHAPTER VI

"SO, what can we do now?" Thania asked in a hushed voice, unable to tear her gaze from the image on the screen. "We certainly can't hope to destroy all of those vessels. Powerful as the *Ultra* is, we'd have no chance of that."

"We could certainly take a lot of them with us," the ever valorous Viona declared.

"We surely could," her mother agreed. "But sometimes expediency is better than foolhardiness. Somehow, I think they knew we were on this planet. It may be that the opening of those doors sent an automatic signal to them, telling them that somehow intruders had penetrated their secret chamber and discovered what's in there. But even if they have spotted us, they're still several million miles away."

"And in the meantime, we just sit here and wait for them to come to us?" There was a trace of resignation in Mexone's voice. "With all those vessels at their command, it won't be long before they find us—no matter where we hide."

"We must do something—I agree," the Amazon replied. "But at the moment, I can think of nothing. We appear to have no alternative but to evade them as long as possible. Space is big and we might be able to split their force into smaller factions and deal with them that way. Whatever happens we fight to the finish."

She looked to her husband for affirmation. Instead, he allowed the onboard computer to take over the controls and walked to the subsidiary console table.

"Did you not hear what I said, Abna?" she asked shortly. "We'll soon have a battle on our hands and you decline to answer me."

Glancing up from the console he said, "Sorry, Vi. But I've just had an idea. It may not work—indeed, it an extremely slim chance we have, but it may just be possible."

Somewhat mollified by his answer, the Amazon joined him at the table as the others crowded round. "What is it you're looking at?"

she asked, as successive star fields flashed up on the viewing screen as Abna punched in instructions at the keyboard.

"Our large-scale star maps of this region. Unless my memory fails me, there was something marked which might just enable us to wipe out that alien fleet of spaceships at a single stroke."

"When you're in a position like this, no plan is without its risks. What do you expect to find on those charts? There's nothing but stars marked."

Abna found the chart he was looking for, and turned up the magnification, running his keen gaze over the thousands of stars depicted there.

"I can't imagine what can possibly be out there which can help us," Viona said, mystified. "Just a multitude of stars of all colors and sizes. We can't hide there for long."

"I'm not looking for a star," Abna told her. "But when we were checking on other stellar systems in this region, I'm sure I noticed something else."

He uttered a sudden exclamation and jabbed his finger at the screen. "I wasn't mistaken. There it is."

"There what is?" Thania inquired: She could see nothing out of the ordinary. "Unless you mean that odd-looking smudge about thirty light years away."

"That's exactly what I do mean. Perhaps you don't know what that smudge represents. It marks the position of a cosmic storm. There are extremely powerful magnetic and electric fields in the galaxy. Fortunately, they're not common and they're usually found acting across regions between the spiral arms. Normally they remain static and, knowing where they are, we can avoid them.

"But sometimes, especially if a very massive sun in the vicinity of one of them explodes as a supernova, the tremendous force of such a detonation will add its own incredible energy to it. Whenever that happens, the storm begins to move and quite often in a manner which is entirely unpredictable. Not only do they move through space but they can also spin and the velocity and direction of that spin depends solely on how close the supernova happens to be and its direction from the storm when it explodes."

"I think I can understand that." Thania nodded. "But how does it help us?" Her eyes widened and her expression suddenly changed to one of undisguised alarm. "You're surely not going to take the *Ultra* into a cosmic storm?"

She turned to where the Amazon was standing nearby. "That would be suicidal, wouldn't it? Even the *Ultra*, powerful as it is, could not survive that!"

The Amazon bit her lower lip in deep thought. Even though Abna must have considered this before even proposing this alternative, she had to agree with the teenager. She had designed and built this vessel and knew its strength—but the thought of taking it into that tremendous mass of almost unbelievable energy, a seething cauldron of high-energy particles traveling at close to the speed of light, shook even her.

Looking up at her husband's thoughtful face, she asked, "Is there something else you haven't told us yet? I don't believe even you would propose such a course without thinking it through."

"No, I wouldn't and as I said earlier, there's only a slim chance of us surviving and, at the same time, destroying that entire armada of spaceships. To put it simply, because it is spinning around an axis, quite often there are holes through these storms. It's rather like the axis of a centrifuge or the eye of a hurricane. The charged particles are flung outward towards the circumference."

"In other words, there is a possible path through such storms," Viona put in, nodding her head. "And you're hoping to steer the *Ultra* through it."

"Not me personally, the onboard computer. Only that can make subtle changes in course sufficiently quickly. But you must take into consideration two things. Firstly, that gap will be extremely small, and it may not be perfectly straight. It could change its direction extremely quickly. And secondly, despite their deadly effects, these storms are virtually invisible. That's why I thought you all ought to know the odds before we decide on such a plan."

There was a painful silence. Then Thania asked, "And just how big are these storms?"

Abna's answer was immediate. "About a few light years in diameter and perhaps forty or fifty light years in length—which means we have to travel through it in the fourth dimension."

Staring out of the observation window at the swiftly approaching fleet of enemy vessels, Mexone asked, "And have you any idea what the effect of that storm will be on the *Ultra*—and ourselves—when we're traveling through hyperspace?"

Clenching her teeth, the Amazon answered him. "We have no idea at all. The *Ultra* has never passed through one of these storms. As Abna rightly said, they're extremely rare. We don't even know if such storms can have any effect at all in hyperspace. As you all know, in the normal course hyperspace is completely isolated from normal space. In it, we can pass safely through even stars and planets. However, Abna believes that in the seething cauldron of an unnatural storm, space itself may be warped, so that there is a possible 'seepage' of energies across dimensions. Such energies, striking the energy field around a ship in hyperspace would overload it and cause it to collapse. The vessel would then be returned to normal space—right into the heart of the storm! All of which is purely theoretical."

"May I suggest we put my proposition to the vote?" Abna interrupted. "There's very little time but the Crusaders are, after all, a democratic group. Each of us is entitled to a say in a matter as serious as this. How many of you are prepared to take this risk—raise your hands if you agree."

Turning, he saw that every hand was raised. Stoutly, Viona said, "We all knew there were risks when we embarked on this mission through the galaxy. I say that if there's only one chance in a thousand that we'll succeed, we should take it—especially if it means destroying most of that arrogant and oppressive race."

"Well said, daughter." The Amazon gave a nod of acquiescence. "Abna and I will make all of the necessary calculations and then feed them into the electronic brains. The rest of you prepare yourselves and also keep a close watch on those vessels out there. If this is to work, we want them to follow us—but not too closely if we're going to lure them into that storm."

Seated at the table, the Amazon and Abna worked through the complicated mathematics, first setting a course for the distant storm, and then feeding in the necessary data concerning the storm itself.

"I'll arrange for the computer to continually update itself as more accurate data comes in once we get close to that area," the Amazon said. "Then it will continually check the particle flux from every direction and make any required adjustments as we enter the storm.

The one unknown factor is whether all of that tremendous energy can have any effect where four-dimensional travel is concerned."

Having designed and built the on-board computer herself, giving it an almost human intelligence coupled with nanosecond responses, she knew that what was being asked of it now was almost at the limit of even its capabilities. Their very lives would depend upon the decisions it would take every ten billionth of a second.

"I'll also put in the spatial coordinates of this sun," Abna punched in the required figures. "We're going to be tens of light years away once we emerge from that storm into normal space and we want to be able to find our way back here."

Finally sitting back in her chair, the Amazon called, "What's happening with the enemy vessels?"

After a brief pause, Viona replied, "They seem to be maintaining their distance, which is surprising. I would have expected them to increase their velocity and try to catch up with us. They must know they have the overwhelming advantage."

"From what I've seen of them, they're one of the most cruel races we've met, without a spark of decency in them," the Amazon remarked. "They are probably playing cat and mouse with us, hoping to prolong the agony on our part."

Taking up the sheets of paper covered with the intricate calculations, she carried them across the room and commenced feeding the numbers into the electronic brains of the computer. Once this was done, she returned to the others. "Everything is ready," she said with a somber note in her voice. "Once we embark on this, there is no turning back. We'll be committing ourselves to possibly the greatest danger we've ever faced."

"I'm ready," Viona declared. Glancing round, she added, "I think we all are."

"Good. Then let's get to it. Now all we need is for that pursuing fleet to rise to the bait. All of you strap yourselves into your couches."

She waited while they were all settled, then threw one last look at the enemy behind them, making sure that now they had been sighted by those on board the enemy spaceships. Lowering herself into her own couch, she fastened the straps rechecked that the course towards the distant storm was correct, then reached out and clicked the switch which gave the computer complete control of the *Ultra*.

Relays clicked and switches moved automatically. The strange red sun fell away with an increasing swiftness as the acceleration increased. It was now an effort for them to breathe as the tremendous pressure passed beyond the limit of normal human bodies.

Faster and ever faster the *Ultra* shot out into the deeps among the stars, its course holding steady, heading for a point still almost thirty light years distant. Behind then, unseen now, the enemy vessels also increased their velocity, intent that their prey would not escape into the infinities of interstellar space.

The Crusaders saw nothing of this. Strapped in the well-upholstered couches their bodies pressed tightly against the springs, they lay unmovable. Then, some five million miles from the red sun, with the velocity almost that of light the four-dimensional energy warp enveloped the *Ultra* and they slipped into hyperspace.

Copper blocks were placed ready to feed themselves automatically into the power unit whenever they were needed. Deep within the ship, the electronic brains functioned with a flawless precision, following the computations which had been meticulously programmed into them.

Ahead of the *Ultra,* in normal space, the raging chaos of the storm lay directly in their path. It had been in existence for more than ten thousand years, gradually building into the monster it had now become. But it had remained stationary, a mass of intermeshing magnetic and electric fields almost beyond comprehension.

Suns in its immediate vicinity all contributed masses of gas in the form of highly ionized atoms, swirling with incredible velocities along the lines of force.

Then it had engulfed the massive star just at the time of the supernova explosion. Now, something more deadly was added—it began to move. Traveling with an incredible speed, its velocity was still far less than that of the light from the supernova which now preceded it. Electrically charged particles moving at near light-velocity, spun and whirled across a diameter of three light years. Half a dozen stars, which had lain in its path, had erupted as normal novae as it engulfed them. Entire planetary systems had been totally obliterated and reduced to mere cinders in the endless dark within this comparatively small region of space.

And it was towards this seething chaos of invisible energy that the *Ultra* was now hurtling, still enveloped within the four-dimensional energy warp. Behind the vessel, the enemy spacecraft had noticed the change and had also switched to hyperdrive, their instruments continually locked onto the *Ultra*.

Moments later, in the four-dimensional continuum, the *Ultra* dived towards the pre-determined point, an exceedingly minute region of calm within the ravening chaos, although still larger than the spaceship itself. Ultra-sensitive instruments monitored the flux of high-energy particles striking the hyperspatial envelope around the vessel, fed the ever-changing data into the computer, constantly altering the course to maintain the huge ship within the region of minimum impacts that represented the only safe course through the storm.

On and on the Ultra traveled, crossing vast distances in a fraction of the time it would have taken traveling in normal space. In a state of unconsciousness, none of the occupants were aware of what was happening. The strident shrilling of the automatic alarm brought both Abna and the Amazon to full consciousness. The Amazon lifted her head to stare around the huge room. The first thing she noticed was that they were no longer in hyperspace.

At some time, the *Ultra* had slipped back into the normal space-time continuum. For a few seconds, she found it impossible to think clearly. The fact that the four-dimensional envelope no longer surrounded the *Ultra* presumably meant that they had exited the storm.

Beside her, Abna too looked bewildered. If everything had functioned perfectly, why had the alarm gone off? Instinctively, he pulled the switch to divert the power from the main drive into the forward rockets, slowing their tremendous velocity.

"What's happening?" Thania cried, loosening the straps and starting up from her seat. "Are we still inside that storm?"

Moving swiftly to the instrument monitoring the external radiation counter, the Amazon checked it carefully. There was a worried expression in her violet eyes as she turned. "There's still an exceptionally high radiation count out there. My guess is that we are approaching the end of it—but still not out of danger. A seepage from the storm must have overloaded our energy warp and cut it off prematurely."

"And from the look of things, we still have plenty of trouble ahead of us," Abna said tautly, a concerned frown on his face. He pointed towards the large visiscreen that now showed a view of normal space. "Take a look at that!"

Almost in the exact center of the screen was a most peculiar object. To the watchers, it looked like a tangled mass of luminous strands, expanding filaments of glowing gas.

"What under creation is it?" Viona gasped. "I've never seen anything like it before. In a way, it looks strangely beautiful."

"Beautiful, perhaps," the Amazon said grimly, "but deadly. Those expanding layers of gas are the remnants of the supernova, moving outward with a velocity of about five thousand miles a second. From the diameter of those filaments, I would say the actual explosion occurred some years ago. That small, brilliant object in the center is what's left of the original massive star.

"It's a sun smaller than Sol but with a surface temperature close on half a million degrees and thirty thousand times more luminous. But there's no time to go into that now. Our velocity is still far too high for us to turn the *Ultra* sufficiently to avoid it. The first thing we have to do is reduce our speed as quickly as possible."

"Even then, it's going to be a tight thing." Abna spoke from in front of the controls. Swiftly, he fed more power to the forward rockets. The engines shrieked as he pushed the power to the limit. Plates creaked around them.

Deep shadows of doubt etched Abna's handsome features. The deceleration tore at their bodies as they stared in awe at the swiftly approaching ring of swirling gas and the glaring, tiny disc in the center.

Tens of thousands of miles fled by with each passing second. Inside the control room, the tremendous strain was beginning to tell on them. Slowly, infinitely slowly, the red needle on the velocity indicator edged down.

"She's still not maneuverable," he said in reply to the Amazon's look of mute inquiry. "I can't get her to turn. Very soon, we may be caught in the gravitational grip of that sun."

"Keep trying." The Amazon forced herself to speak casually. She knew that Abna was doing everything possible—that if anyone, apart from herself, could get them out of this danger, he could.

The radiation indicators now told them that the danger from the dregs of the storm was lessening swiftly. The *Ultra* had survived one of its most perilous journeys. Now, all they had to do was get their incredible velocity down to the point where Abna could turn the nose away from their present course.

The blazing disc of the supernova remnant now dominated everything on the viewing screen, an intense white orb surrounding by the glowing tendrils of gas that had been ejected at the moment of the explosion.

Then, very slowly, the disc began drifting to the right, away from the center of the screen. Strain still showing on his face, Abna grunted, "I think we're going to make it. I've fed as much power as I dare into the forward rockets. Any more and the engines are going to overload."

"I'll check that the anti-radiation screens are at maximum power," Viona called.

The *Ultra* was now beginning to move diagonally, away from the sun but their course was going to take them through part of the surrounding gas cloud with its associated pressure wave.

A short while later, there was a tremendous jolt. Had they not been prepared for it, and hanging on tightly, they would all have been thrown to the floor. Great sheets of glowing hydrogen gas swirled around the ship, almost blinding them,

Narrowing his eyes, Abna kept his glance fixed on the instruments, checking on the amount of high-velocity particles outside the vessel. Plates creaked—but still the shield held. Then, miraculously, they were through and slowly withdrawing from the vicinity of the fiery remnant.

Abna turned the *Ultra* through a wide arc until it was pointing in the direction from which they had come. Very gradually, he slowed the vessel until they were almost motionless in space.

Going over to the observation window, the Amazon stood with her hands clasped tightly behind her, staring out into space in the direction of the retreating cosmic storm. "Very soon, we'll see if we've succeeded in destroying that enemy fleet."

"You seem so sure they will have followed us into that storm," Mexone remarked. "It could be they were also aware of its existence and position. If they did, surely they wouldn't be so stupid as to follow us."

"You're thinking that if they came from some other stellar system they would surely be aware of it?"

"Well, it's quite possible," Viona added. "We've found no other planet in that other system where they could have come from. Yet you now seem certain they don't originate from some planet of another sun. What makes you so sure?"

"I have my reasons," the Amazon replied enigmatically. "If they don't emerge from that storm yonder within half an hour, I'll know I'm right."

Half an hour passed—and then another. Still there was no sign of anything appearing in the vicinity of the supernova remnant. Finally, the Amazon was satisfied. "That tells me everything I want to know," she said. "Those spaceships are finished. Whatever is left of them is trapped inside that storm. We can return to that other planetary system now."

With the spatial coordinates already fed into the computer, the *Ultra* made a smooth turn onto a course that would take them well clear of the cosmic storm. Taking their places again, Abna set the switches that would increase their velocity to an appreciable fraction of the speed of light before the energy warp came on and they slipped smoothly into four-dimensional space.

CHAPTER VII

FROM a distance of fifty million miles, the stellar system looked exactly as they had left it. Nothing had changed with the exception that the enemy space armada was no longer there. By now, they were all certain that their plan had worked. Whether that had been all of the vessels the enemy possessed was something they did not know.

The *Ultra* had left four-dimensional space five minutes earlier by their chronometers and now they were reducing their velocity as the curiously pulsating sun and its two attendant planets showed directly ahead.

Turning in his chair, Abna said, "Now that we've arrived back, Vi, suppose you tell us why you're so certain this race is indigenous to this system. We've already ruled out those two planets as being the worlds of their origin. So where exactly do they come from?"

In answer, the Amazon got to her feet and pointed directly at the sun. "They come from there," she said sharply. The note of conviction in her voice was unmistakable.

The other Crusaders stared at her as if she had temporarily lost her senses. Shaking her head uncertainly, Viona said, "You think this race is living inside that sun! But that's impossible. All right, I know that Idron and his people live inside the shell of that outer planet but from what we saw there, that's perfectly feasible. But inside a sun!"

"I know it sounds ridiculous but it's the only possible place."

"Which leaves us with the one thing you haven't considered, Vi," Abna commented. "Although the surface temperature of that sun is at the lower end for stars, the temperature inside must be well over twenty thousand degrees. How can anyone possibly live under such conditions?"

The Amazon tightened her lips in exasperation. "I'll grant you that under normal circumstances it's something I wouldn't even consider. But here we have a race with a technology capable of building that time machine we found on the jungle planet. If they're at the scientific level necessary to construct something like that, it's not impossible they could surround a dense core, made from that material they're stealing from the outer planet, within a stable bubble of much cooler gases while the rest of the solar furnace goes on around them."

"Even so it would take an almost impossible amount of energy," Viona remarked. "Where could they possibly get so much colossal power?"

The Amazon was silent for a while, waiting to see if any of the others could make a suggestion. When none was forthcoming, she went on, "I would have thought it obvious since it's the answer to this puzzle. They get it from the sun itself. It's the reason why they have speeded up time around this sun."

A silent moment, then Viona said excitedly, "Of course. Just like a beating heart, those rapid oscillations are pumping energy back into the sun all the time."

Abna's puzzled face cleared. "You're right of course, Vi—just as you usually are. So what are we going to do about it?"

The Amazon studied the distant sun for a few moments before answering, "I think we should take a look at what this other world looks like. If those other vessels can fly in and out of it at will, I'm sure the *Ultra* can."

"Unless they have some form of shielding which protects them from the intense heat," Mexone cautioned.

"That's possible. But I think it is a risk we must take. Once we know for certain what we're dealing with we can find some method of eliminating this cruel race forever."

As the Amazon moved towards the controls, Thania said, "There's one thing I don't quite understand, Amazon."

"What's that, Thania?" The Amazon spoke without turning her head.

"If this region where time is speeded up only operates around the sun, why don't we see that sun behaving normally when we're well away from it in outer space?"

"That a good question. The answer, of course, is that light isn't affected by time at all. It always travels with the same velocity. The only difference we see is that slight fuzziness we noticed earlier."

Taking over the controls, the Amazon fed more power to the engines and turned the *Ultra* slowly until the nose was pointing directly at the sun. Beside her, Abna pressed a small button. A few seconds later, darkened, radiation-proof screens slid over the windows and large visiscreen.

With the much-reduced brightness, they were able to pick out small details as they speared through space, the image of the sun growing larger with every passing second. Several dark sunspots were clearly visible, and a large prominence showed to one side, a huge jet of gas rising swiftly, high above the surface.

Beyond the hull of the *Ultra*, the protective screen was already in place. Swiftly, the image of the sun filled the entire forward viewing screens. It seemed that nothing else in the whole universe existed. Twisted tongues of red flame leapt up to meet them. Even with the protection of the screen, the temperature inside the control room began to rise.

With one hand, the Amazon wiped away the sweat from her forehead to prevent it dripping into her eyes. Narrowing her eyes, she peered into the screen, searching desperately for something other than the seething chaos of ionized atoms that made up the sun's outer surface. Her task was made even more difficult by the way the sun was behaving.

One minute they were in space and the next they were enveloped in fire. Had it not been for the tremendous power of the engines, they would have been tossed back and forth like a bottle on the ocean. Still, she kept the *Ultra* on course. Then, a little way to one side, she made out what she was looking for. In certain aspects, it was similar to that hidden world inside the outer planet.

But this was not a pleasant sight. A dark sphere showed on the screen. It was about the size of Earth's moon, possibly somewhat smaller, its surface lit by the raging turmoil within the sun's interior. Even as she headed the *Ultra* towards it, she made out the shimmering glow, like a weird atmosphere, which surrounded it.

"You were right, Vi," Abna said. "That looks like some kind of planetary cooling unit. Are you going to take the *Ultra* inside it? It's just possible our approach has been seen and they'll know immediately this is not one of their vessels."

Grimly, the Amazon nodded. "My guess is that since this is an artificial planet, it's probably highly unstable."

"So perhaps a handful of super-x-hydrogen bombs might be enough to explode it completely?" Mexone suggested.

The Amazon considered that for a minute, still keeping her attention on the fast-approaching counterfeit world. "We can certainly try that," she agreed finally. "Right now, I think we should be prepared for some kind of attack. I've no doubt they may have some kind of ground missile launchers down there."

Moments later, they entered the glimmering outer zone around the planet. As they had figured earlier, the outside temperature now commenced to fall. A thousand miles away, the stone-and-metal core hung suspended within the nuclear furnace inside the sun.

"I can see flashes," Thania yelled excitedly. "They're firing at us."

The impacts came several minutes later. Several shocks jolted through the *Ultra* but the screen held and the Amazon kept them on course. "Prepare to fire those bombs," she ordered tersely. "I think it's time they discovered the kind of armaments we have. We don't want to be too close if the bombs have the effect we hope."

"At least there's no sign of any spaceships. They must have sent every single one they had after us." Viona gripped the edge of the controls hard as more explosions hammered against the shield.

At a nod from the Amazon, Abna tripped the switch that sent eight super-x-hydrogen bombs spearing down towards the planet. All were aimed at the same spot and programmed to explode immediately on impact.

In the control room, the Crusaders watched breathlessly not quite knowing what to expect. They were still several hundred miles from the planet and it would take a little time for the bombs to reach their target.

Then the impact on the planetary surface came. It began as an expanding orange glow as all eight warheads detonated simultaneously. The brilliant flash of that tremendous explosion spread swiftly. What happened next was something the Crusaders had never witnessed before.

The entire world split open down the middle like an apple cleaved with a knife.

Blindingly brilliant light, though only just a little more intense than the brightness inside the sun flared across their vision. Disintegrating rapidly, large chunks of the stricken planet hurtled in all directions.

At the controls, the Amazon said harshly, "It's time we got out of here. Hold on. This is not going to be easy or pleasant."

Minutes passed as she turned the *Ultra* in a tight arc and sent it hurtling back through the outer layers of the sun towards empty space; minutes of strain and wondering if that colossal energy wave produced by the total disruption of the planet would catch up with them before they could get free. They were also pulling against the powerful gravitational grip of the sun itself.

Metal plates creaked and groaned around them. Needles danced on the various instruments as waves of electrically charged particles hammered against the hull.

Then, finally, they were through. Behind them, the sun diminished slowly in size.

Ahead of them lay the black, eternal deeps of space.

Slowly, they forced taut muscles to relax and sat back as the Amazon put the *Ultra* on automatic control. Running a slim hand through her blonde hair, the Amazon said quietly, "Now there's only one thing left for us to do—destroy that time-distortion machine on that primeval world. Once that is done, everything should return to normal in this system."

"Is that absolutely necessary?" Mexone queried. "After all, there's nothing for either those cave-dwellers or Idron's people to fear now with that race wiped out."

"That's true—but something tells me it has to be destroyed. When anyone starts tinkering with time it can lead to disastrous results. There's no way of telling whether other races might visit this planetary system just as we did and their intentions might not be as benign as ours. All it's doing now is keeping that sun in its highly abnormal state."

Without any further words, she set the course for the distant planet.

CHAPTER VIII

FOUR hours later, they landed on the smooth plateau facing the high escarpment The huge doors were still open but there was no sign of the body of the alien they had left lying on the ground in front of them.

Mystified, Thania stared through the observation window at the spot where he had been. "What can have happened to him? Surely none of those aboriginals would come here just to remove his body."

"Nor would any of his friends," Mexone put in. "As far as we know they never came back here."

"Aren't you forgetting the other inhabitants of this planet?" the Amazon said, with a grim smile on her lips.

"The other inhabitants?" Thania asked.

"Those huge carnivores. They would make short work of him if they happened this way."

"Of course." Satisfied, Thania gave a nod. "You think they might also have gone in there?" She indicated the wide-open metal doors.

"There's nothing in there for them. I think we'll find everything exactly as we left it."

Which is what they discovered when they went inside a short while later. Still functioning perfectly, the spinning tesseract in the center of the machine drew their gaze towards it, twisting their vision as they tried to follow its sight-wrenching motion.

Switching her attention to the pedestal and then the large snaking cables coming out of the walls, the Amazon made a brief, but complete, assessment of the situation.

Watching her, guessing at the thoughts running through her mind, Abna said, "Whatever method we use to destroy this, it will have to be thorough. We have no idea what this metal is, or what effect any explosive will have on that curious hazy shield around this machine."

"It may be that even a nuclear device will have no effect," Viona said, eyeing the machine. "Even if we pulled all of the cables out that would be only a temporary measure."

"Could we not run a cable from the *Ultra's* power drive and overload that thing with atomic energy, just as we did using heat with those ice creatures?" Thania suggested.

After a reflective pause, the Amazon shook her head. "That's a good suggestion, Thania—but it's out of the question I'm afraid."

"Why?" The teenager looked disappointed.

"It might destroy this machine eventually but before that happened the initial effect would be to speed up those solar oscillations even further. We would literally tear that sun apart and I want to avoid that at all costs. It would mean the end of all life on these two planets."

"Then if atomics are out—what else is there?" Abna said tensely. "Do we try ordinary explosives?"

"That might work," the Amazon said musingly. "If not, there's only one other way."

"Which is?" Mexone asked.

"The way we first defeated those ice creatures—sheer brute force."

Thania stared at the madly whirling machine, a look of concern on her face. "You mean we simply smash it with our bare hands?"

"Not exactly," the Amazon corrected. "First we'll try high explosives. Two of you bring some from the *Ultra*, together with a timing device."

The others waited while Mexone and Thania went back to the *Ultra*. A few minutes later, Thania reappeared in the airlock carrying a heavy wooden box in one hand. Slowly, she began to descend the ladder and in that same moment, the ground shook.

Swiftly, the Crusaders inside the chamber ran to the doors. "What is it—an earthquake?" Viona gasped.

The Amazon stared at the dense jungle at the far end of the plateau. "Not an earthquake," she answered. "It would seem we have visitors." She pointed.

Three gigantic armored shapes came thundering out of the jungle trees. Ear-splitting roars echoed into the distance.

Drawing themselves back into the entrance, they withdrew their weapons. Thania had already seen the danger and was clambering back inside the *Ultra*. A second later, the airlock slammed shut behind her.

The Amazon breathed a sigh of relief. "At least they're safe," she said tautly. Aiming swiftly at the first dinosaur as it came charging across the hard ground, she fired. The bolt of searing energy struck the armor-plated hide. The monstrous beast uttered a thunderous shriek of agony but still came on.

Behind it, the remaining two charged straight for the opening in the cliff. By now, Abna and Viona were firing rapidly, sending blast after blast at the creatures. Having no knowledge of fear, Viona deliberately stepped into the middle of the opening between the doors and took careful aim.

She aimed directly at the massive hind leg of one of the creatures. Great chunks of scaled flesh and bone flew from the limb and the monster teetered for a moment and then went down. A second shot hit the threshing head between the glaring eyes. Jerking spasmodically, the dinosaur slumped, twitched violently for a few seconds and then lay still.

Towering more than thirty feet into the air, the other two still came on. Twin rows of foot-long teeth lined the gaping jaws. Edging forward a little way, Abna sent a searing blast at one of them. The fearsome head exploded as the blast found its target. Even though it was dead on its feet, the creature continued forward for several yards before crashing against the high wall of the cliff twenty yards away.

The third, however, came straight for the open doors. Without pausing to think, the Amazon leapt forward, grabbed Viona around the waist, sweeping the girl off her feet and carrying her to the comparative safety of the interior of the chamber.

The next second, a monstrous head was thrust through the opening. Lunging forward from the side of the opening, Abna thrust his blaster hard against the creature as the gaping jaws turned on him. In spite of his enormous strength, the massive head knocked him sideways before he could fire, slamming him against the wall.

A razor-sharp tooth sliced down the side of his leg, ripping the flesh. With a wild cry, Viona regained her balance. A scything blast cut across the dinosaur's neck. With a deafening cry, the head withdrew. For a moment, the tremendous bulk of the creature completely blocked the exit. Then it crashed onto the ground outside.

Running forward, the Amazon went down on one knee beside Abna. "How bad is it?" she asked anxiously.

"Just ripped the flesh," he replied. "I'll be all right in a few minutes. Are all of those beasts dead?"

"Every one of them," Viona told him as she looked concernedly at the gaping wound. Changing the subject, she asked, "You don't think those fangs carry poison?"

Shaking his head, Abna concentrated his metaphysical powers on the gaping sound. It was the Amazon who said, "I doubt if that wound is poisoned, Viona. They may be carnivores but from what I've learned from Earth's prehistory, they aren't venomous."

By the time Mexone and Thania joined them, the wound in Abna's leg was completely healed without even a scar to show where it had been.

Thania lowered the heavy box to the floor and pulled off the lid revealing several sticks of explosive.

"Right," said the Amazon briskly. "Let's get this explosive in place, set the timer, and then see what happens."

It was the work of a few minutes to strap the explosive to the pedestal just beneath the time machine and set the timing device. Once she had checked it carefully, the Amazon followed the others and hurried from the chamber. Running across the open ground, they took shelter behind the massive bulk of the *Ultra.*

Five minutes later, the explosive detonated with a cavernous roar. It was followed by the rumble of falling rock. A cloud of white dust puffed out between the doors and quickly dissipated.

They approached the opening cautiously in case any more rock was about to fall. Heaps of rubble lay around the machine and more had fallen just outside. But they doors were entirely undamaged and as the veil of dust settled they saw to their disappointment that the pedestal and time-warp generator were both intact. The powerful explosive had had no effect!

"What now?" Mexone asked dully. "It seems we'll have to use a nuclear device and hope that this machine doesn't absorb more atomic energy and shatter that sun to pieces."

"There's one more thing we can try before we have to resort to that," The Amazon declared. "As I said earlier, we try sheer brute force."

"But if the high explosive has no effect, how—?"

"I suggest we bring the portable projectile launcher from the *Ultra* and fire an armor-piercing rocket exactly at this strange shield of energy. If we can perforate it, there's just a chance the rocket will hit that tesseract—which I suspect is highly unstable."

"I suppose it's worth a try," Abna acquiesced. "It will only take a few minutes to set it up. We'll need to be a safe distance away. We've no idea what will happen if this succeeds. We'll use a telescopic sight to align the rocket accurately."

The launcher was set up on the very edge of the plateau some three hundred yards from the chamber. Very carefully, peering through the small telescope, and slowly turning the controls, the Amazon aligned the rocket at the point where she knew the spinning tesseract was situated behind the shield.

"Everything ready," she called a moment later. "I suggest we all take shelter among the trees and hope there are no more predators in the vicinity."

Moments later they were crouched down among the massive trees trunks as the Amazon prepared to fire the rocket electrically. Deliberately, she flicked the switch. The rocket fired immediately, spearing towards the gap between the heavy metal doors.

As straight as an arrow, it struck the whirling shield of energy. The next instant, the crusaders were temporarily blinding by a brilliant flash. Then there came a low rumble. When they could see again, the entire side of the cliff had collapsed inward, burying everything.

Slowly, the Amazon got to her feet. A few feet away, Thania rubbed her eyes as green after-images danced in front of her vision.

Abna was shaking his head slowly. "I'm not exactly sure what happened, but from what I see there, that entire chamber imploded, pulling the cliff down with it. I think that we should—"

He stopped his flow of words instantly as once more the ground shuddered beneath their feet. Unable to remain upright, the Crusaders fell to the ground, their entire bodies shaking with the shocks. Several of the tall trees swayed and then crashed to the ground.

"It's an earthquake—and a big one," Viona gasped as she struggled to steady herself. "It feels as if the whole planet is shaking."

"We have to make it to the *Ultra* and try to take off." The Amazon spoke through tightly-clenched teeth. "Even the ship might not be able to take much more of this."

Already, the *Ultra*, huge as it was, was swaying slightly as further concussive waves struck. Using all her strength to combat the endless shuddering, the Amazon managed to stand on her feet. Together with Abna, she grabbed the others, holding them tightly and pulling them forward.

More trees fell as they hauled themselves up the swaying ladder and into the airlock. Leaving the Amazon to close the doors, Abna ran to the control room. With an effort, he lowered himself into his seat, his fingers moving swiftly over the levers as he started the engines.

Staggering from side to side, scarcely able to keep their balance, the others threw themselves down into the chairs and strapped themselves in. "Prepare for take-off," Abna said tightly. Without waiting for any reply, he threw the switch that transferred the power to the jets.

The *Ultra* began to rise, slowly at first and then with increasing acceleration, streaking through the turbulent cloud layer towards space. Minutes later, they broke through the atmosphere. Stars in their thousands glittered all around them.

Only then did they relax and take time to glance at the sun, staring at it in utter amazement. Now it shone with its normal red color, utterly quiescent, with no sign of any of its former pulsations! It was no different from any other sun.

Surprise was mirrored on Viona's face as she said, "It doesn't seem to be pulsating at all. What can have happened? Certainly it seems we succeeded in destroying that alien machine but I thought that once that happened it would go back to be a normal pulsating star."

"That is what would normally have happened," the Amazon explained. "But all the time that time was speeded up by the machine, the rate of evolution of the star was also increased tremendously. It went through that unstable phase of its career very quickly so that now it's reached the point where it's completely stable."

She made to say something more but at that moment, Thania, standing near the opposite window called, "Look! Something is happening to that outer planet. It seems to be getting bigger!"

The others went over to join her. The disc of the planet was clearly visible again the teeming thousands of stars. What Thania had said was evidently true. The planetary disc was steadily increasing in size.

"So that is what all that commotion was about on this world. I thought it was an earthquake caused by the implosion inside that chamber. It seems I was wrong. It was a planetquake."

"I don't understand." Thania turned to face her, incomprehension on her face.

"Somehow, when that time bubble around the sun collapsed, it caused a tremendous gravitational change in this system. Time can do strange things when you try to change it. Somehow, it always stabilizes itself.

"And in this case, it's normalizing everything. There must have been tremendous gravitational stresses caused when those aliens first formed that time sphere around this sun. Now they're being smoothed out, bringing that outer planet back to its original orbit—a circular one nearer the sun."

"Then that will mean its atmosphere will form again—and the end of those ice creatures," Thania exclaimed.

"Almost certainly it will," Abna agreed, bringing the *Ultra* to a virtual 'standstill' now they were sufficiently far in space to safely view all that was happening. Glancing at the Amazon, he said quietly, "Well, it looks as though our task here is finished. You've solved the mystery of that sun and everything seems to be getting back to normal."

"So it would seem," the Amazon agreed. The distant world was moving swiftly now, far more quickly that before. "It will probably take weeks for that world to settle into its new orbit closer to this sun and then everything will be as it was before those aggressors came."

Shortly thereafter with an increasing velocity, the *Ultra* headed outward into the galactic deeps. Ahead of them, a tiny cluster of multi-colored stars shone like a galactic jewel against the eternal dark.

www.ingramcontent.com/pod-product-compliance
Lightning Source LLC
Chambersburg PA
CBHW011518170626
46810CB00009B/3403